CINDER

www.chellebliss.com
CHELLE BLISS
USA TODAY BESTSELLING AUTHOR

COPYRIGHT @ 2023 BLISS INK

Publisher © Chelle Bliss October 3rd 2023
Edited by Lisa A. Hollett
Proofread by Read By Rose & Shelley Carlton
Cover Design © Chelle Bliss
Cover Photo © Michelle Lancaster @lanefotograf

www.chellebliss.com
CHELLE BLISS
USA TODAY BESTSELLING AUTHOR

MEN OF INKED: HEATWAVE SERIES

Book 1 - Flame
Book 2 - Burn
Book 3 - Wildfire
Book 4 - Blaze
Book 5 - Ignite
Book 6 - Spark
Book 7 - Ember
Book 8 - Singe
Book 9 - Ashes
Book 10 - Scorch
Book 11 - Torch
Book 12 - Inferno
Book 13 - Cinder
Book 14 - Dare

To learn more,
please visit *menofinked.com/heatwave-series*

*

CHAPTER 1
ASHER

"BLESS YOUR HEART," my grammy says to the cashier as she counts the change wrong for the third time. "Keep the change, honey."

"Are you sure, ma'am?" The cute girl looks dumbfounded.

"Yes, child. I'm sure," Grammy Washington says, smiling sweetly—although she's anything but, especially when people aren't bright.

I grab the bags, heading toward the door with grammy at my side.

"The girl's lucky she was born with beauty. She sure didn't get an ounce of brains," Grammy says, hoisting her purse strap onto her shoulder.

"That's not very nice, Grammy."

"I said she was beautiful."

"And dumb," I remind her.

She shrugs as she wobbles next to me as we walk

toward my truck. "We can't all have everything, baby. But I'm telling you right now, always go for brains first and beauty second. Looks change. Smarts don't."

"Asher? Asher Gallo?" a female voice calls out, making me turn my head.

"Sweet baby Jesus," my grammy mutters. "Here we go."

That's when I see her. A girl I haven't seen in a handful of years, and the last time I laid eyes on her, she was nowhere near as stunning as she is now. "Asher. Oh my God. Asher. Look at you," she says, rushing up to me and throwing her arms around me.

"Olive?" I whisper, unable to stop myself from hugging her back, even with my hands full of groceries.

I knew Olive Thornberry for the first sixteen years of my life, but then her family moved away, and I haven't seen or talked to her since.

"I've missed you," she breathes into my ear, sending goose bumps scattering across my skin even under the sweltering rays of the sun.

"You too, Olive," I say to her, pulling away to get a better look at her face but regretting the loss of contact at the same time. "What are you doing in town?"

"I've been staying at my grandparents' while they're on a cruise, to check out the USF campus for grad school, but I'm heading back tomorrow," she blurts out, barely taking a breath.

"Grad school?"

She nods, beaming with so much pride. "I got accepted into a medical research program there and start this fall. I'm pursuing my doctorate."

"A smart one," Grammy says, elbowing me in the ribs. "Beauty too."

I ignore my grandmother and keep my focus on the beautiful brunette in front of me. "That's impressive."

Olive shrugs like it's no big deal, but it very much is. "It'll only be impressive if I can finish the program. Getting in isn't the hardest part."

"I'm sure you'll kill it."

"Enough about me. How are you?" she asks, her eyes roaming away from my face. "You look…" She smiles softly, soaking me in. "…well."

"Kids today," Grammy whispers under her breath behind me. "Asher, do you mind if I wait in the car while you two catch up? It's too hot out here for an old woman such as myself."

I look back and down at my short little grandmother, wiping the sweat from her brow. "Sorry, Grammy. Let me get the door for you."

I pull the key fob from my pocket and start the truck, unlocking the door. "Give me a minute," I tell Olive before helping grammy.

Grammy leans over as soon as she takes my arm. "Invite her over."

"What?" I ask, shocked because grammy doesn't

like any woman I'm even remotely interested in, and most certainly doesn't ask for them to come by when we're about to have a family celebration. "Are you serious?"

She peers up at me, staring into my eyes with so much seriousness. "Do I ever joke?"

She has a point. The woman is as serious as they come and has only grown more serious with age. "Not really. You say it straight, Grammy."

"Ask Kalamata over for dinner."

"Olive, Grammy."

"That's what I said," she tells me like she's in the right, when she very much isn't. "Ask her over. Do not let that one walk away without setting, at the very least, a date."

"I don't think—"

"You never think when it comes to women, child. Maybe for once, you should. Listen to me when I tell you, do not let her walk away. I see the way she looks at you and the way you look at her. That doesn't happen every day."

"What look?"

"Men are clueless beasts," she says to herself as she climbs up into my pickup truck, holding the grab bar and sliding in like she's done it a million times. "Now, go. I don't have all day. We have food to finish."

I set the groceries in the back before leaving grammy in the air-conditioned truck. I don't need to turn around to know Grammy's watching us, judging my every movement, and probably having an entire conversation with herself about what a dumbass walking hormone I am at this point.

Olive's exactly where I left her, fiddling with the hem of her flowery sundress and staring at me. She's no longer the awkward teenager with braces and long, skinny arms. "Your gram seems nice."

"Seems is the operative word."

Olive laughs, and the sound is utterly beautiful. "I'm sure she's not that bad."

"She is. Trust me. She's the devil in disguise."

"I think all older women are," she says, touching my arm and instantly sending shock waves through my system.

I ignore the sensation, knowing my dick has a mind of its own. "If you're not doing anything today, you can find out for yourself. We're having a little party at her house in a few hours, but no pressure if you're busy."

"I'm sure she has enough mouths to feed without adding another."

"Don't be silly. She insisted that I ask you."

Olive turns her green-eyed gaze toward my truck. "She wants me to come?"

"She does."

She blinks, looking shocked. "Why?"

"A pretty girl with brains. Killer combination."

Olive laughs again. "We're not uncommon, Asher."

I tuck my hands into my pockets, knowing exactly what kind of women I have been hanging out with, and it's not the brainiacs. "Never said you were, Oli. Anyway, I'd love to catch up and hear about school and your family. Maybe think about dropping by, and you can watch the devil in action."

She holds out her hand. "Give me your phone."

I don't even hesitate to pull it from my back pocket, unlock it, and hand it over to her. Spending the evening talking to Olive will be better than anything else I'd do for the evening. I've heard every story, listened to the same complaining about the exact same topics over and over again. It's mind-numbing.

Her phone dings in her back pocket. "I have your number, and now, you have mine. Text me the address, and I'll drop by later. What can I bring?"

"Can you cook?"

"Asher Gallo. I'm a good Southern girl. Of course I can cook, and I do it well."

The girl is getting more and more perfect, and maybe it's seeing her after so many years, but now I wonder why we never dated. "Bring anything you want. Whatever you have time for, or just bring yourself. We always have tons of food. Too much, really."

"Hush it. There's no such thing as too much food."

"I hope you like to eat, then."

"I do."

"Asher, time's slipping!" Grammy yells from the truck before slamming her door.

"The devil calls," I say to Olive. "See you later, then?"

"I wouldn't miss it for the world," she tells me, and for the first time in years, I'm excited about the possibilities.

CHAPTER 2
OLIVE

"ASHER GALLO?" my brother asks like he didn't hear me right the first time I said his name.

"Yeah, dummy. I ran into him in the grocery store parking lot."

"It's a no for me, sis. Sorry, but he isn't right for you."

I glare at the phone, wishing River could see my face. "One, it's not your decision who I see or have dinner with. Two, there's absolutely nothing wrong with Asher."

River blows out a breath on the other end of the phone. "I'm older and wiser than you are, and there's absolutely a lot wrong with Asher when it comes to you."

I chuckle loudly because although he is older, there's nothing wise about my brother. He's not unintelligent, but he's led around more by his dick than his brains. "Do we really want to compare smarts?"

"You were too busy studying to pay any attention. He was a hound dog in high school, and his present-day probably isn't much different if the man is still flying solo."

River acts like I'm clueless. Asher and I ran in the same crowd, although I was more of a wallflower than an active member of the group. I wasn't boy crazy, looking for attention from anyone. I spent more time studying and at home than out partying with the rest of the group. When we moved, I left all my friends behind and never settled into a new group at my new high school.

"Were you ever an angel, Riv?"

"You know I'm a dog, Oli. I've never hid that from anyone, including women, and especially not from you. But Asher is…"

"Choose your words very carefully," I warn him, gathering up the plate of fried green tomatoes and homemade dip I just finished making. "The man was with his grandmother at the grocery store on a Saturday. He was kind to me and didn't stare at me like I was a piece of meat. He had manners and sweetness."

"They're all sweet until they get in your pants."

"You're not sweet to anyone," I remind him.

"Just be careful, sis. I don't want you to get your heart broken again, and a man like Asher Gallo could easily do that to a girl like you."

"A girl like me?"

I hate where he's going with this entire conversation. He's shit-talking Asher, a man he hasn't seen in almost a decade and barely knew in high school. And now he's ripping into me, implying that I'm weak and gullible.

"You fall easy and fast. You're not as experienced as other people. And with how things ended with Chris…"

Chris, the bastard. He was a self-absorbed, egotistical maniac who spent more time staring at himself in the mirror than holding a conversation. I was smitten with him at first, drawn to his good looks and high-class upbringing. I thought he liked me… loved me, even, but it's hard to love someone else when you're too in love with yourself. I found him sleeping with my roommate at the end of last semester, and I ended things on the spot.

"I warned you about Chris, but you said I just didn't understand him. I may not understand you, but one thing I understand completely is how a man's mind works."

"I won't start planning our wedding. Happy?"

"It's a start, but don't expect—"

"I'm expecting a kick-ass meal and catching up

with an old friend. Nothing more. Nothing less. Can you treat me like an adult instead of a dumb teenager?"

River sighs. "I said what I needed to say."

"And it was too much."

"I'm sorry, Oli. I'm just trying to protect you."

"It's not your job. I'm a grown-ass woman. Bad shit's going to happen in my life. I'll survive. I don't try to micromanage your life. Do I?"

"No," he grumbles.

"I should, though. Because, quite honestly, it's a shitshow."

"Hey now."

"Where's the lie?"

"I got to run."

"Of course you do."

"Aren't you late?"

I look at the clock on my phone and instantly break out in a cold sweat. "I am. Fuck."

"Have fun, sis."

"Bye, Riv."

We hang up, and I race around the kitchen, grabbing my purse, keys, phone, and the bomb-ass fried green tomatoes and dip before heading out the door.

Ten minutes later, I'm standing in front of the old Washington house that doesn't look so old anymore. It's freshly painted the most beautiful shade of grayish baby blue. There are so many cars on the street and in the driveway, I take a step back, debating running away instead of going inside.

"Shit," I mutter. "There're so many people."

The front door opens, and Asher stands tall, filling the doorway. "You came," he says, looking every bit as handsome and sexy as he did earlier.

Time has been good to him. His hair is a little longer than in high school. The perfect length to run my hands through. And his lips…

"Let me get that," he says, waking me from my daydream and snapping me back into reality as he takes the plate from my hands.

"Thanks," I say, my voice hoarse and way too needy for my liking. "The house is stunning."

Asher stops moving, looking up at the house, and he smiles, making my insides go all soft. "I painted it a few weeks ago. I wasn't sure about the color, but now that it's up there, I think it was a perfect choice. Grammy sometimes has good taste."

"That must've been a lot of work."

He starts to walk toward the door, and I hang back, using the opportunity to check out his body and his ultra-fine behind. The man is tall and lean, without an ounce of fat. He's not overly muscular, but I'd have no problem feeling protected while wrapped in his arms.

"Only took me a weekend. It made grammy happy and was totally worth it."

God. He's sweet. I don't care what my brother says or how Asher was in high school. He's not the same man now. And he's nothing like Chris, who wouldn't spend an hour helping a family member, never mind giving up an entire weekend.

When our feet touch the front porch, Asher turns to face me, looking serious. "I'm sure this is going to be a bit different from your family's dinners."

"We don't do dinners with my family, Asher. I have no frame of reference."

His eyes darken as the tiny, almost invisible lines on his forehead become more pronounced. "What do you mean, you don't do dinners?"

"It's always been just the four of us since we moved—and even before that. My grandparents were never the family-dinner type. They never liked company, and I'm honestly shocked they let me stay at their place while I visited USF. They don't like people in their space, even their own."

Asher stares at me with his mouth slightly open. "Not even their own grandkids?"

I shake my head. "Nope. If it weren't for visiting my mom's side of the family up in Georgia a few times a year, I wouldn't really know any of my family."

"That's sad. I can't imagine my grandparents, on both sides, being anything other than welcoming. So, prepare yourself to be completely overwhelmed. And when it becomes too much, let me know, and I'll get you out of there."

"I'll be fine. It'll be fine," I say, not knowing if I'm trying to convince myself or him.

He gives me another soft smile as he touches my upper arm for a moment. "I'm serious, Olive. When it's too much, tell me. My family can be a lot, and they're nosy too."

"Unlike my family, I love people, Asher. I'm sure I won't need a rescue."

"I warned you," he teases and follows those words with a wink. "Stick close."

He reaches for the handle, and I brace myself for whatever insanity is on the other side. But nothing could have prepared me for the large number of people talking and laughing, which is completely opposite of my father's family.

I follow him inside, and my feet stop moving along with the rest of me. I do my best to soak in the scene before me.

Asher grabs my hand, easing me out of the entryway. "You good?"

The house is filled with so much energy, I feel the love deep down in my core.

"Perfect," I say, unable to stop a smile from spreading across my face. "They sound so…"

"Loud."

"No. They're happy. It's love."

"Kalamata," his grandmother says, coming toward me with open arms.

Kalamata? I'm not even annoyed, although I should be. "Hi, Mrs. Washington. Thank you for having me."

"Ruth, please," she says while hugging me. "You're a bag of bones. Asher, make sure she eats something. No one leaves hungry."

"I'm so sorry," Asher says as soon as his gram leaves us. "I don't know why she calls you that."

"It's okay."

"It's not okay. She's being feisty, and it's not nice."

"I've been called worse."

His eyebrows rise, and his eyes flash. "Like what?"

"Show me around," I tell him, changing the subject. "I am a little hungry too."

Asher wastes no time taking me into the kitchen, where there're so many plates on the counter, I'd swear this was a buffet and not a family dinner party. He places my fried green tomatoes in the only empty spot and uncovers them. "These look amazing."

"They're nothing compared to all this food."

He hands me a plate and starts dishing out the food, quickly filling up the entire thing. "Grammy said to feed you, so I'm feeding you."

"I can't eat all this," I say, watching as he drops a helping of potato salad onto my dish.

"Whatever you can't eat, I'll finish. If your plate isn't full, grammy will have my hide."

He not only fills my plate but makes one for himself, before we head outside, finding two spots at a long table filled with his family underneath a tree for shade.

"Asher, who's your friend?" an old man asks as he sips on a glass of wine.

"This is Olive, my old friend from high school."

"Ah, Kalamata."

"Uncle Denzel," Asher warns.

The old man laughs. "I know it's Olive. I'm sorry, dear. Forgive me."

"There's nothing to forgive," I say as I take a bite of my first forkful of food.

"Don't excuse his behavior," Asher tells me as he stabs at the food on his plate. "He knows better."

"I do," Denzel says. "But I think the name is cute. It fits you."

"How in the hell does it fit her?" Asher asks, holding his fork above his plate and staring at his uncle with such intensity I hold my breath.

Denzel places his wineglass on the table and settles into his chair. "Olive sounds like an old lady, but Kalamata is a special type of olive. And there's something about her that tells me she's not ordinary."

"She isn't ordinary," Asher replies. "Olive is anything but ordinary."

Heat climbs up my throat, settling on my face. "You don't know that. We haven't seen each other since we were sixteen," I say.

Asher turns his gaze toward me, his golden-brown eyes shining bright. “You weren’t ordinary then either, Olive.”

CHAPTER 3
ASHER

"DON'T LET that one get away," my uncle whispers in my ear, leaning over me as he gets up from the table.

I peer up at him and nod before turning back toward Olive, who's deep in conversation with my aunt Brenda.

"Prince is truly the most revolutionary musician of the twentieth century."

"Who?" Olive asks, looking confused.

"Dear God," I mutter, shaking my head.

My aunt Brenda is and always has been obsessed with Prince. She mourned his death for months by wearing black like she'd lost a member of her family.

"Child, you don't know who Prince is?" Aunt Brenda asks.

Olive shakes her head. "My parents were into

classical music, and nothing else was played in our house."

"We must change that," Aunt Brenda says, pulling out her phone and typing away on the screen.

A few seconds later, Prince's "Sexy M.F." is blaring at full volume.

"Listen to the genius," Brenda says, bobbing her head to the beat. "I lived for this song."

"The man wore high heels," another man tells her, making fun of my aunt, but she waves him off. "Seriously, Brenda. He was like a garden gnome."

"Hush it, Fred. Pocket men are sexy too."

"Pocket men?" Olive asks, almost choking on her food. "What the…"

Brenda giggles with a nod. "The man was five foot two of pure sexiness. If he'd wanted to slide into my pocket, I would've happily accommodated him."

"This isn't even his best song." Fred shakes his head. "And he was a chick singer."

"A chick singer?"

"He only made music for the ladies."

"I am a lady," Aunt Brenda tells him.

"Debatable," Fred mutters.

Brenda raises an eyebrow, staring down Fred, who's not a relative but a friend of the family who's always around.

Fred coughs, knowing Brenda could easily put him in his place, and if Denzel overheard, there would be a problem.

"I'm going to get more food. Anyone need anything?" Fred asks, pushing himself up from the table.

"Don't hurry back," Aunt Brenda says.

Fred grumbles under his breath as he walks away.

"Don't you just love this song?" Aunt Brenda asks Olive.

"It's different, for sure," Olive says.

"Olive, I want to show you something," I say, needing to get away from my aunt before she forces us to listen to another golden oldie.

"Okay," Olive says, smiling at me and knowing exactly what I'm up to.

This is a rescue operation for the two of us.

I help her from the table, tucking her hand into the crook of my arm. "Sorry about that."

Olive leans her body toward mine. "Don't be sorry. I liked the song."

"Don't ever repeat those words, or you'll be stuck listening to Prince for hours. Which means I'll be stuck listening to him for hours too."

Olive laughs. "There are worse things."

"The only upside is I'd be doing it with you, but I'd rather be talking than listening to old songs and hearing my aunt reminisce about the olden days."

We find a private spot in the backyard and sit on the grass, our legs touching. "Are you going to USF for sure?" I ask, curious if she's coming back for good.

"I got accepted already. I start this fall, and I

wanted to see about housing and if I wanted to live on campus or not."

"And what did you decide?"

"I don't want to live with a bunch of fresh college kids. I'm going to grab an apartment near campus, but far enough away I don't have to listen to endless parties on the weekend."

"Smart," I tell her, resisting the urge to haul her into my lap and kiss her.

I'd be lying if I didn't confess, at least to myself, that I've thought about kissing Olive before. In high school, the girl was drop-dead gorgeous but hid behind a pair of big, black-rimmed glasses and usually had her face buried in a book.

"What are you studying exactly?"

"Neurology."

"Wow." I suddenly feel inadequate with my work in tattooing. "That's impressive."

"It's exciting. USF has a research clinic dedicated to the study of Parkinson's and Ataxia. I'll be joining the research team there while I work on my doctorate."

My entire body rocks back. "Ataxia?"

Olive nods. "It's very rare. Have you heard of it?"

"Heard of it? Hell, Olive. My grandfather had Ataxia."

Her eyebrows rise. "What? Really?"

I nod. "He died before I was born, though. My mom was tested a long time ago for the gene, but luckily, she doesn't have it and neither does anyone else in the family. We dodged a bullet."

"Oh, thank God. It's an awful disease."

I sit there, still in shock. "What are the odds that's your field of specialty? We'll have to tell my grandmother. She'll be even more in love with you than she already is."

"And you?" she asks, looking at me in such a way that I know she's as into me as I am her.

"I've always liked you, Olive."

"I liked you too," she admits, unable to meet my eyes.

I reach over, placing my fingers under her chin, and tip her head so her eyes meet mine. "I like you more now than I did then."

"You do?" she asks, sounding genuinely surprised.

"I do," I tell her, not breaking our eye and physical contact.

Her eyes are a stunning green, framed by her deep auburn hair and fair skin, dotted with freckles. "But you're you."

"And?"

"And I'm me."

"What's that mean?"

"You're cool, and I'm not," she explains.

I smile, loving that she thinks I'm cool, but loving even more that she thinks she's not. "Babe, you're the perfect package."

She stares at me, not blinking and barely breathing. "I'm not perfect."

"In my eyes, you are."

"I'm a nerd."

"Brains are sexy," I tell her, loving that she's smarter than me.

She runs her hand up my arm, her fingertips gliding over my ink. "You'll grow bored of me."

"Do you want to find out?" I ask her, moving closer so I see nothing except her, and she only sees me.

"I do," she breathes, staring at me with so much need. "But don't break my heart."

"If anything, you're going to break mine," I tell her, leaning forward until our lips touch.

The kiss is whisper-soft and filled with possibility. I don't push it, don't go deeper, wanting to give her something to look forward to. But in the process, I know my fate is sealed as electricity courses through my system from the simple, innocent kiss.

Olive Thornberry is meant to be mine.

CHAPTER 4
OLIVE

MY MIND IS BUZZING with possibilities after kissing Asher Gallo. Never in my wildest dreams, even after he invited me here, did I think he'd actually kiss me, let alone be interested in me.

But with school coming up this fall, I'll need to spend more time studying my books than memorizing the planes of Asher's body. Maybe he wouldn't break my heart. I don't have time for complications. I've never been the type of woman who could keep things casual, but maybe this time could be different.

Asher's next to me as we walk around the backyard of his grandmother's house. "Who's that?" I ask after my eyes land on a man who's both beautiful and scary at the same time. He's sitting near Brenda, concentrating on a giant plate of food while she talks to him.

"Mammoth."

"Okay," I draw out because he didn't quite answer my question, at least not in a way that would fill in any missing blanks. "And he's…"

"Tamara's husband."

"Oh, wow." I'm impressed with Tamara. I always thought she liked the clean-shaven pretty boys. I would've never guessed she'd end up with a man so rough-looking.

And right on cue, Tamara comes walking out of the house, holding a plate of food and two beers. She looks as beautiful as ever. When we were younger, I wanted to be her. She was everything I wasn't and knew I'd never be. Besides her beauty, which was off the charts, she was loud, bold, and unapologetically herself. No one messed with Tamara Gallo if they had any brains, and I envied her for her ability to take no bullshit.

"She looks so good," I tell him as we walk their way.

"She's all right. She'll be happy to see you."

"I don't think she'll remember…"

"Olive. Oh my God. Olive Thornberry," Tamara says, sliding her plate onto the table next to her hunky husband before setting down the two beers.

I swallow, hating to be the center of attention, but it's too late. I already am. Not only are her eyes on me, so are her husband's and half the party's.

"Hi," I squeak out, earning myself a squeeze of my hand from Asher.

"Breathe, Olive. It's only Tamara," he says, like he has the ability to read my mind.

Tamara's in front of me before I have a chance to fully fill my lungs. She throws her arms around me, hugging me like I'm a long-lost relative she hasn't seen in forever. "Fuck, girl. You're a sight for sore eyes."

I hug Tamara back with one hand, Asher refusing to let go of me even when she pulled me into a hug. "You look amazing," I tell her, but Tamara's never had an ugly day in her life. "You haven't aged a bit."

Tamara pulls back and gives me a once-over. "Damn, you grew up, girl. You didn't just grow up. You had an entire glow-up."

My face heats at her compliment. "I don't think…"

"Shush it. Accept the compliment. Soak that in. Remember it. You're fucking beautiful, Olive. Baby," Tamara says, turning her head toward her husband, "this is Olive, an old friend from high school."

"Hey," he says with a lift of his chin between bites of some of the best-tasting macaroni and cheese I've ever had in my entire life. He's a man of few words, but that's okay. I imagine beautiful people don't need to say much to get and maintain attention.

Tamara rolls her eyes, swiping her hand through the air in his direction. "Ignore him. He's hangry. And when the man is hangry, there's nothing on his mind except food. I mean, he's sitting there listening to Brenda as she rambles on about Prince, and he's completely unfazed as long as he has something left on his plate."

"I swear, the man has more patience than most nuns I know," Asher tells his sister. "Because food or no food, I can only take Brenda in small doses."

"Oh, it won't last long. I give him another five minutes before he walks off unless I sit down next to him and immerse myself in Brenda's world of music."

I smile, loving the easiness of everybody here. I would listen to Brenda for hours as she rambles on about Prince over the sorry state of affairs with my family.

"Come sit with us," Tamara says. "We have so much to catch up on."

Asher looks at me, waiting for me to give the thumbs-up or down.

"Sure," I tell her, smiling at Asher. "If that's okay with you?"

"Fucking great," Tamara says, peeling away to walk toward her husband.

"If it becomes too much, let me know, and we'll leave."

"No," I say to him as we walk toward the table and the two open seats near Tamara and Mammoth. "It's not too much." Nothing could be more than what I've already been through, especially the Prince marathon Brenda subjected me to.

"You've been warned," he mutters before I settle into a chair near his sister. "I'm going to grab us some drinks." Asher gazes at his sister until she looks up at him. "Behave."

She jerks her head back, looking at him like he's a moron. "Go, Ash. I'm not going to do anything except catch up with an old friend."

Tamara and I were never friends. I knew her because of hanging out with Asher and his friends, but I was never cool enough for Tamara. She hung around with her cousins and a few other people, but I never had enough of an outgoing personality not to be swallowed whole by them.

As soon as Asher walks away, Tamara shakes her head. "He's being weird."

"Men," I mutter like I have absolutely any clue about how Asher normally acts.

"What are you doing here?"

"Asher invited me."

Tamara shakes her head. "No, babe. What are you doing in Tampa? Didn't you move away like forever ago?"

"Ten years ago," I say, running my palms across the tops of my legs. "I was visiting USF. I'll be attending there in the fall as a grad student."

"Holy shit. You're still fucking smart."

I don't bother to tell her it's not something a person usually loses. "Sometimes."

"Babe," Tamara says as she smacks her husband's ink-covered bicep with the back of her hand. "Olive was the smartest girl in school."

"Impressive," he says, but I can tell he's barely listening. He's too busy concentrating on his plate, but I don't blame him. Our conversation isn't entirely penis-worthy.

"Grad school," she breathes. "I'm not even surprised."

"Thanks," I say, but I'm not sure that's the correct response. If it isn't, Tamara doesn't let on.

"And River?" she asks. No one around here has forgotten my brother. He's unforgettable in the same way Asher and Tamara are. Beautiful people are rarely forgotten, especially ones with outgoing personalities. "Is he well?"

Tamara and River were never a couple, but they did flirt relentlessly throughout high school. I always thought they'd go out, but it never happened. My brother was too much into keeping his options open, and Tamara made it known she'd never date anyone from our high school. She didn't want the gossip mill to have any more ammunition than it already did. I couldn't blame her. I felt the same way she did, but no one bothered to show much interest in me. I was too busy with my nose stuck in a book to even see if any boy was giving me the time of day.

"He's really good. He lives in New York City and is a stockbroker."

"Not surprising," she says, nodding slowly with a smile. "It's the perfect job for someone like River."

"He's great at it."

"I'm sure," she says before taking a long pull of her beer.

"What'd I miss?" Asher says as he places two beer bottles on the table in front of us before sitting down next to me.

"Not much," I tell him.

"Did she behave?" He stares at his sister when he asks that, getting himself a sticky mac and cheese noodle thrown in his direction as a response.

"I always behave."

Mammoth grunts, clearly listening to our conversation even if he's not engaging with us.

"How did you two hook up?" she asks.

"We didn't hook up," I'm quick to say.

"We ran into each other when I took Grammy to the store this morning."

"Interesting," Tamara mutters. "And you invited her?"

"Grammy insisted, and I'm damn glad she did," he tells his sister.

Tamara turns her head to where her grandmother is seated, in a heated conversation. "Grammy? Really?"

"Yep," Asher snaps.

"Fucking bananas," Tamara adds.

"Right?" he asks her.

"What's bananas about it?" I ask them.

They share a look, one only a brother and sister could understand. River and I do the same thing, and it annoys the hell out of people. Sitting here, watching them do it, I completely understand why.

"Grammy doesn't like anyone," Tamara explains. "No girl is good enough for her Asher."

"College girl," Asher says, tilting his head my way. "Brains and beauty."

It's the first time Asher has ever called me beautiful, and I'm not even lying when I say it does wonders for my soul and ego. My heart practically skips a beat, and the small amount of humid air inside my lungs gets lodged there.

"Amen to that," Tamara says, picking up a noodle from Mammoth's plate when he isn't looking. "How long are you in town for, Olive?"

"I'm heading back tomorrow, but I'll be here permanently this fall."

"That's brilliant," she says. "I'm glad you'll be sticking around."

"Me too," Asher says, making my already erratic pulse become even more unstable.

"What song next, guys?" Brenda asks us, oblivious to our entire conversation.

"'Purple Rain,'" Tamara answers, casting me a smile.

"Oh. One of my favorites." Brenda smiles as she taps away on her phone before the song starts to play.

"I bought us more time, and FYI, they're all her favorites."

I chuckle at the statement because in the little time

I've known Brenda, I've already caught on to that fact.

"Do you have to find a job while you're in school? I know a few people down in Tampa who may have some side work if you're interested."

"I'm good," I tell her, having saved as much money as I possibly could over the years to fill in any gaps. "I am lucky enough to have a scholarship to cover tuition, and my parents are taking care of the rest."

"Nice," she says.

"I'm lucky."

"Nah, babe. It's not luck when someone is as smart as you. It's all hard work and genetics."

"Mostly hard work," I tell her, knowing my parents had nothing to do with all that I've earned. If I hadn't spent the last ten years buried between the pages of every book I could get my hands on, I wouldn't be where I am now.

Tamara snorts. "You always were the bookish type."

High school me would've taken some sort of offense to her statement, pulling back into my little protective shell. But the me of today, the one who's going to grad school with dreams of my PhD, I couldn't care less. I wear that statement like a badge of honor.

"I wish I were as smart as you, but no matter how

many books I could ever read in my life, I'd never come close," Tamara adds.

"That ain't no lie," Asher says in a teasing tone.

"Hey," she says with a glare. "You're not an Einstein either, brother."

"I know things. I read way more than you ever have, Tam, but I knew what I was going to do with the rest of my life, and college wasn't in the cards."

"What are you doing?" I ask him.

"I work at Inked."

"He does the most delicate line work you've ever seen in your entire life. It's so fucking weird," Tamara adds.

"I love that you followed your passion."

In high school, besides chasing women, Asher was constantly drawing. The man always had a pencil in his hand, scribbling on anything and everything he could get his hands on. I envied his creativity. He could turn a blank piece of paper into the most beautiful piece of art.

Asher slides his hand around the back of my chair, his fingertips coming to rest against my bare shoulder. "I always knew what I wanted to be and that we were someday going to take over the family shop."

I have to remind myself to breathe as Asher touches me in the lightest way possible, sending goose bumps all across my skin. "You two work together?" I ask Tamara.

"Oh, hell no. I got a degree in graphic design, and

I own my own company. Tattooing flesh wasn't in the cards for me."

"She has a thing about blood," Asher adds.

A little girl in the frilliest dress comes barreling in our direction with a melting popsicle in her hands and matching blue streaks down the front of her. "Mama, look what Granny gave me." She thrusts the popsicle in Tamara's direction, looking so damn proud of her treat.

"Oh, that's great, Riley. Is it delicious?" She pulls the little girl into her lap, not the least bit fazed by the possible mess.

"Blueberry," the little girl says before going to town on the frozen dessert.

"Come here, sweetheart." Mammoth grabs the girl off Tamara's lap, taking the brunt of the melting popsicle, leaving his wife unscathed. "Give me some of that. Daddy's hot."

"In more ways than one," Tamara mumbles, giving her husband a wink.

He smiles at her, and my heart almost stops. The way he looks at her…he's in total and complete love with her.

"This is Riley," Tamara tells me, dipping her head toward the little girl on Mammoth's lap. "She's the youngest. Jackson's around here somewhere, but good luck getting him to stay in one spot for more than a few seconds."

"He's like his old man," Mammoth says, looking

every bit the proud papa with a giant smile before he takes a hearty bite out of Riley's popsicle.

"Daddy, don't eat too much," Riley squeals, trying to pull the popsicle back from Mammoth's face.

"I'm sure Grammy has another one," he tells her before giving in and letting his daughter have the rest.

"I'll get you a red one," she says, wiggling off his lap and running away so fast, I'm sure her little legs might give out.

"Kids," Tamara mumbles. "Do you have any?"

"Me?" I touch my chest, a little shocked by the question. I don't know if anyone has ever asked me that before. Maybe it's because none of the friends I hang out with in school have kids. I don't run with a mom crowd.

She nods, waiting patiently for my response. "Oh, no. No kids for me."

"Ever?" she quickly asks.

"Someday."

"There's no rush." Asher runs his fingertips across the back of my shoulder. "She has a degree to finish first."

"Exactly." I turn to him, unable to stop myself from smiling. "As soon as I'm done with school and find someone who wants to be my baby daddy."

Asher smirks. "I know someone who can fill that position."

"Oh, sweet Jesus," Mammoth mutters. "Lame."

My face heats, and I don't need a mirror to know

my entire top half is bright red. "I'll put you at the top of my list, Asher Gallo."

He curls his hand gently around my deltoid as he looks me straight in the eye and says something I never thought I'd ever hear, "I want my name to be the only name on that list, Olive."

CHAPTER 5
ASHER

"LOCK IT DOWN," Mammoth says to me as my sister and Olive walk toward the house, leaving us behind.

"What?" I'm barely paying attention to him, too focused on Olive and the way her fine ass moves when she walks. She's mint.

"Lock her down," he repeats, his voice more gravelly this time because he's annoyed that he had to repeat himself.

When they disappear into the house, I turn my attention toward my brother-in-law. "Dude, I haven't seen her in almost ten years."

He's taking a sip of his beer, but he has one eyebrow raised. "So?" he grumbles against the rim of the bottle.

"So," I repeat.

He wipes his lips with the back of his hand,

always classy. When my sister said she was marrying the guy, I was shocked as shit because he wasn't the type I thought she'd end up with. "What the hell does that have to do with locking her down?"

I rub my forehead, trying to hold at bay the headache he's causing me. "We barely know each other."

Mammoth rolls his eyes, a thing he clearly picked up from my sister. "You like her?"

"Yeah."

"Is she smart?"

"Well, duh."

"Is she pretty?"

I throw my arm out toward the house, waving my hand. "You've seen her."

Those words are met with another grunt. "Is she needy?"

I lift a shoulder. "Don't fucking know that yet."

"You want to put babies inside her?"

"I...uh..." I did say that. Damn. I told her to put my name on the list and make sure it was the only damn one on there too. I have never said that to anyone, nor have I wanted to, but here I am—words spoken, and I can't take them back. But that's the funny thing; I don't want to.

Mammoth leans forward, placing his elbows on the table as he wraps a hand around the beer bottle. "Lock her down, or else you're going to lose her."

"She can't walk away from this."

Mammoth laughs as he shakes his head. "Kid got more ego than smarts."

"I'm not an idiot, brother, but Olive's different."

"Different how?"

I shrug.

"She got tits?"

I nod.

"She pretty?"

I nod again, but we've been over this.

"She make you want to be a better man?"

I pause for a minute, thinking about his question. I'm different around her, even when we were in high school. I'm nicer, more thoughtful. Something other women have complained about. I'm always down for a good time and deliver more orgasms than most men, but after that, I'm not interested in getting to know the woman. I have one goal, and relationships have never been it.

He leans back in his chair, spreading his legs apart, looking totally at ease and like he's been a member of this family his entire life. "There's your answer."

"To what?"

"Your sister made me want to be a better man."

"And?" I swear the guy talks in riddles sometimes. I haven't been able to determine whether he's brilliant or a lucky moron who stumbled into the best shit of his life.

"When a woman makes you want to be the best version of yourself, she's the one."

"She's the one?" I ask, but I don't know if I'm talking to him or me. "It's been a few hours. She could be totally bananas, and I wouldn't know yet."

"Spoiler alert, dumbass. All women are bananas, but don't lie to yourself and think you're normal. You have more than a few screws loose up in that dome of yours."

"I'm completely sane and normal."

Mammoth tips his head back, laughing so hard, he holds his stomach. Asshole. "There isn't a normal damn thing about you, Ash."

"Oh, like you're the pillar of sanity."

He laughs harder. "I'm fucking whacked, but I'm honest with myself, and your sister accepts me for the hot mess I am."

"Because she's bananas too. I grew up with her, and I know she's a little off most of the time."

He wipes his eyes from where he laughed so hard, he made himself cry. But then he sobers, clearing his throat a few times before he speaks. "Together, we center each other. Somehow, when we're together, we are normal… Don't ask me how, but it fucking works."

"Whatever," I mumble, but even together, they're nothing close to normal. But if they were, they would be completely boring.

"You're a fool if you let that smart girl get away.

When she starts school this fall and is surrounded by a bunch of horny dudes, pursuing their doctorates, you're going to lose out on the best damn thing in your life. It's now or never, brother. Shit or get off the pot. Lock her down, and you can breathe easy."

The sliding door opens, and Tamara and Olive walk out, laughing about something and looking like they're best friends.

"Tamara likes her."

"Tamara doesn't know her."

"Your sister can tell if a person is shit as soon as she meets them. She has a freakish ability to nail someone's personality within minutes. Look at them." He pauses, but I'm already looking and soaking in the ease of their interaction. "She's a good apple."

"She was wrong about you, and then there's Crow."

Mammoth grumbles under his breath that I'm an absolute asshole. "Crow's not a bad person. Shit judgment sometimes, but not an asshole."

That may be the first time I've heard him say anything nice about Crow, the guy my sister was into and meant to be with when she ran headfirst into Mammoth and never looked back. I'm thankful for that too. Mammoth is perfect for my sister, and Crow, while probably not a shit human, has a record after serving time in prison for manslaughter.

"Hey," Tamara says, staring at me with her face all scrunched up. "What's the face for?"

"The face?" I ask, dropping whatever look I had that got her attention.

"You look funny. What were you two talking about?"

Olive slides into the chair next to me with a plate of cut-up fruit in her hand. "You okay?"

"I'm great," I tell Olive before turning my attention toward my sister. "It's just my face, Tam."

"It was uglier than usual," she says, snorting at the funny she made. "And more serious."

"We were just talking shit, babe. Man things," Mammoth says to her, taking the beers from her hands and setting them in the center of the table.

"So sorry we missed that snooze fest," she says, teasingly. "Were you talking about ball scratching and engine size?"

Mammoth slides his chair closer to my sister, moving his arm to the back of her chair. "Baby, there's only one engine you need to worry about."

"You two are going to make me puke. Like for real, for real."

"For real?" Tamara asks me, unfazed by her husband's lame attempt at coming on to her.

"Who wants to hear the *Crystal Ball* album?" Brenda asks us.

We'd completely forgotten she was sitting here. The music just became part of the background, and she didn't say a word while Tamara and Olive were gone. I'm sure she listened to everything, probably filing it away to gossip about later.

"It's completely underrated, but there are great songs on it."

"Yeah," Tamara tells her, taking the path of least resistance. "Put anything on."

I glare at my sister, hating when she feeds into Aunt Brenda's abnormal obsession that, somehow, we all have to suffer through.

"What do you have to do before fall?" Tamara asks Olive, ignoring the hate I'm throwing her way.

"Just find a place to live. Everything else is done."

"Organized," I say. "I like that."

"I'm a planner. Always have been. Always will be."

"She's a grown-up," Tamara tells me, but I know it's a dig at me and how I, in her eyes, often still act like a child.

I turn my gaze toward Mammoth, and he mouths, "Lock her down."

Being the adult that I am, I scratch my nose with my middle finger, making sure Mammoth sees and understands.

Tamara's phone buzzes, and she glances down. "Ma and Pop are here."

"Aw, I haven't seen them in a long time," Olive says.

"Ma's going to be happy to see you," Tamara says. "She always liked you."

But I know what's coming. Ma's going to squeal with delight and then do everything in her power, including her wicked mom pushy voodoo, to get Olive and me together.

"Really?" Olive asks, but it's not surprising at all, even though my mom doesn't like too many people. Just like my sister, my mom can figure a person out in minutes.

But there isn't anything to dislike about Olive. There never has been, and I can't imagine there ever would be.

"Finally," Uncle Denzel says when my parents make an appearance in the backyard. "I thought you were going to ditch us." He leans forward, giving my mother a kiss on the cheek.

"I never miss a party here," she tells him, doing her best to remain cordial with her brother, who is sometimes combative, especially with his sister.

"Anthony." Uncle Denzel gives my father a chin lift but no kiss. There's never been a ton of love between the two, but I don't totally understand why.

"Denzel," my father replies, giving the same chin lift to his brother-in-law.

Ma's gaze moves around the backyard until her eyes land on us. "Excuse me, Denzel. I'm going to go see the kids. They've been waiting for us."

"We all have," Denzel says, but my mother ignores him as she walks away and heads right for us.

"Hey," Ma says with my father right behind her,

not bothering to stick around to chat with Denzel. "Sorry we're late. Your father had…" Ma looks at Olive, and her voice dies.

"Ma, you remember Olive Thornberry," I say to her, because I know she's processing the face, trying to remember her name.

"Oh my God. The cute little bookworm," Ma says, a wide smile spreading across her face.

"That's me," Olive replies, not the least bit fazed by the generalization.

"My God, it's been…" Ma stops talking.

"Almost ten years," Olive answers.

"You're more beautiful than ever, and I don't even know how that's possible because you were stunning even as a teenager."

Olive turns pink at my mother's words. "Thank you."

"Anthony, look it's Olive," Ma says to Pop.

"Figured that out, sweetheart," he says to Ma, earning himself a smack in the middle of his chest from the back of her hand.

"Kalamata!" grammy yells across the backyard, motioning in our direction. "I need you."

"Who's Kalamata?" my mom asks, turning her confused gaze from us to my grandma. "Does she need an old-age home?"

Tamara laughs. "Nah, Ma. It's what she calls Olive."

Ma rolls her eyes. "Why does she have to be so

spicy? She knows this girl's name. God, she's insufferable sometimes." My mother turns her entire body toward my grandmother. "Her name is Olive, Ma."

My grammy waves my mother's comment away. "I'll only keep her a minute."

Olive starts to stand, but I grab her hand, wanting her to know she doesn't have to do anything she doesn't want to. "You don't have to go. I'll go help her."

Olive squeezes my hand and smiles at me. "I like your gram. I'm more than happy to help her."

"Oh boy," Mammoth grumbles. "This is going to hurt."

"If I don't see you in five minutes, I'm coming in after you," I tell Olive.

"I'll be fine," she reassures me before turning her attention toward everybody else. "Excuse me. I'll be back."

"Don't let that old bat scare you away," my dad says, and while Ma laughs, she also gives him another whack. "Hey. You know I love her."

"You aren't going to be breathing for too long if she hears you call her that," Ma warns him.

"She loves me. I can do no wrong in that woman's eyes."

Ma sighs as she sits down in Olive's chair and stares right at me. "I want all the details. How did this happen?"

"We ran into her at the store."

"We?"

"Gram and I."

"Okay, and…?"

"Grammy said to invite her," I tell her.

"She clearly hasn't lost all her marbles," Pop says after he pulls over a chair and sits down next to Ma.

"Why is Olive here…in Tampa?" Ma asks, glossing over my father's comment.

"School. She's starting USF in the fall, working on her graduate studies."

"No shit," Ma whispers, totally impressed.

"Yeah, and get this, she's specializing in Parkinson's and Ataxia."

Ma's eyes widen. "Wait, what?"

I nod. "For real. She told me that was her specialty and that she was going to be working at their research center downtown."

"That's so…uncanny, really. Isn't it? Weird," Ma says, looking a bit rattled.

"She's so smart, Ma. Smarter than I remember," I say, glancing at the house, where Olive just disappeared with my gram.

"Lock her down," Pop says, sounding exactly like Mammoth.

"She's still in school," I tell him.

Pop slowly shakes his head. "Grad school. Totally different. You lock her down and put a ring on that finger. A man like you isn't ever going to do better than her."

"Thanks for the kind words."

"Son, you're ridiculously handsome, just like your old man, but women like Olive and your mother don't come along every day. And if we're not careful, they'll slip right through our fingers. You have to be more assertive. You have to be aggressive. If you like her at all, you lock her down."

"Ridiculous," I mutter.

Ma places her hand over mine on top of the table. "I'm going to agree with your father. We're not saying you need to get married, but you need to take your head out of your ass and make that girl yours. I never claimed you were my brightest child," she says, somehow delivering an insult in the nicest way possible, "but now's your chance to shine."

"Maybe she doesn't want to be locked down," I say, to my ma and everyone else.

That statement is met with chuckles.

"Man, he's not bright at all," Tamara says.

"Honey," Ma says, patting my hand like she did when I was little and she was about to deliver a statement I wouldn't like to hear or would hurt. "If you don't at least have a plan in place to make that woman yours before she returns this fall, you risk missing out on possibly the best thing in your life. The fact that you're even entertaining this conversation, something you wouldn't have stood for in regard to any of those bimbos you brought home before…"

I don't stop her to argue that the other women weren't bimbos. They just didn't have what I needed to keep my attention for more than sex. They tried. Oh, how they tried, but they never stuck. There was nothing about them that was unforgettable.

"Tells me everything I need to know. You've always liked Olive, and now's your chance to follow through and see where it leads you. Lock her down," she adds, driving the nail home.

"I'll lock her down," I say and am met with a mini-celebration so as not to draw too much attention from the rest of the party.

"Time's ticking," Pop says, and I suddenly begin to sweat.

CHAPTER 6
OLIVE

I BARELY HAVE my pajamas on when there's a knock at the door. I race to the living room to peek out the window.

To my surprise, Asher's outside, hands tucked into his pockets, talking to himself. I stare at him for a moment, trying to read his lips, but I fail. Is he giving himself a pep talk? He's so freaking adorable and vulnerable, something I never thought I'd think about him.

He pulls one hand out of his pocket, lifting his arm to knock again when I finally move my feet.

"Hey," I say as soon as the door is open enough to see his face. "What are you doing here?"

"I'm sorry." He looks around. "I should've called first."

"No," I blurt out, leaning against the door. "It's okay."

His gaze travels down my body, getting a good look at my completely unsexy pajamas.

I don't even have time to be embarrassed by the fact that my nightshirt has little kittens and rainbows.

"Never thought someone could look so fuckin' hot in something like that. You could make a dishrag look good."

I push away my mortification and cross my arms over my chest. "I wouldn't say that."

Asher's grin is easy and sinful. "I would and did."

Now's my chance, before I leave until I finish undergrad this spring. The last thing I want to do is blow it. "Do you want to come in?"

"I don't know," he says. "Do you want me to? I can totally go. I just wanted to say goodbye one more time and make sure you're really going to call me."

"I'll call," I reassure him. "I promise. And yes, I want you to come in." I back up, making room for him to step inside.

It's now or never, Olive. You can do this. You've wanted to lay one hot and heavy on Asher since you were a teenager, and now's the moment.

If I don't, it may never happen. The plane could go down on my way home, and I'd never know the sheer pleasure of making out with a man as hot as Asher Gallo.

So, I do what any smart girl would do and launch myself at him as soon as the door closes. Asher staggers back, but his arms are around me, and he's hauling me upward without skipping a beat.

Our lips collide, and I swear I almost break a tooth, but that doesn't stop me from going for it. Asher doesn't stop either.

His body is hard and warm, the perfect combination. I feel small in his arms and light as a feather as he holds me against him, kissing me roughly.

My breath catches in my throat as my body tingles, loving the way he kisses me. No one's ever manhandled me, taking complete control of the situation.

He takes a few steps before falling backward onto the couch, taking me with him. I land with a bounce, slamming my middle against his cock, and I gasp against his lips.

"Wait," I whisper, pulling my face away from his, breaking the kiss. "I…I…" I stare at him, suddenly feeling like an idiot because I'm ruining everything.

But the last thing I want is to be a notch on his belt or another nameless woman he's slept with.

He's breathing heavily, staring up at me with a soft look. "It's okay, Olive. We don't need to rush."

"Are you sure?" I ask, trying to ignore his rock-hard cock pressing against me. "You won't hate me?"

He lifts his hand, cradling my cheek. "I could never hate you, and I'm completely sure. I'll wait for as long as you need to feel this is the right choice for you."

"Why are you so sweet?"

He smiles at me as he strokes my cheek with his thumb. "I'm not sweet, but if I were an asshole to women, my sister would beat my ass."

I laugh, imagining his older sister doing just that. "She can be scary sometimes."

"You have no idea," he says with a small laugh. "You'll be back in the fall, right?"

I nod.

"We'll finish what we started then, but only if you're still into me."

His statement is ridiculous. I've been into Asher Gallo since my boobs started to develop. No amount of time could pass that would make those teenage-girl-crush feelings disappear.

"I'll still be into you."

"You could fall in love before then."

"That's not happening, Asher. I'm too busy with school to even think about men…and they're not you."

"I'd wait a lifetime for you, Olive," he tells me, and if I weren't already completely smitten, I would be now.

Do I think he's sincere? Yes. Do I think he'd actually wait a lifetime for a woman like me? Doubtful. But the thought is nice, even if it's impossible.

I push off him and situate myself on the couch next to him. "I don't expect you to wait for me. Three months is a long time."

Asher rights himself and faces me. "You're going to be gone for three months?"

"That's when school starts."

"Don't you want to come earlier and get settled?"

I pull down the edge of my nightgown to cover my knees, something I do when I'm overly nervous. Well, that and bite a single nail, but that's something I do in extreme circumstances and only when I'm alone. "Maybe," I draw out, unable to meet his eyes because there's nothing else in the world I'd rather do this summer than spend it with Asher.

Asher reaches forward, placing the length of his finger under my chin and lifting my gaze to his. "Imagine the summer we could have…the beach, the sun, the freedom to do whatever we want before you start school. You've worked hard for so many years and deserve a break. Come back early, and we'll make it a summer to remember."

"You really want this?" I ask, still shocked to be having this conversation. Actually, I'm shocked to be having any conversation with Asher, especially one discussing the future.

Maybe he's changed. The guy I knew in high school wouldn't be waiting around for any woman, especially me. Not that I'm not a great catch, because

I am, but because he's not known for waiting, and he was always into girls who were a little more…easy.

He leans forward, and I close my eyes, waiting for his lips to press hard against mine. But to my surprise, his kiss is whisper-soft. "I want this," he murmurs against my mouth. "All of this."

I let my eyes flutter open, finding Asher staring at me. "Okay," I whisper, unable to speak any louder.

The man has quite literally stolen my breath with his sweet tenderness. Something I never imagined him being able to pull off.

I stare at him, unable to take my eyes off him. He's changed a lot since the last time I saw him. He's grown more handsome, which I wouldn't have thought possible. His jawline has become more pronounced and is covered with more stubble than he ever had in high school. It helps make him look older and more rugged. His hazel eyes seem to change by the moment. His lips…his lips were built for kissing.

"Olive, you look like you want to eat me," he says, pulling me out of my thoughts.

"I… Well…" God, I do want to kiss him.

I want to do more than kiss him. I fantasized about Asher when I was younger, and no doubt, he'll be the central player in every one going forward.

"I'm going to kiss you," he says, searching my eyes for approval.

Right now, I'm a puddle of goo. With Asher

holding my chin, our eyes locked, and only inches apart, I'd let him do about anything to me.

Maybe I am already asleep and this is a dream. That would make sense. Maybe the only thing that makes sense. The entire day had been taking place inside my head, and I'll wake up, back in my grandparents' house, alone.

It's not that I don't deserve a man like Asher. I'm pretty, and add in my brains, and I'm the complete package. It's just that this is Asher. A person I've lusted after for so long. When I knew him, I was in my awkward teenage phase with big glasses and braces.

"Olive," Asher says when I don't respond. "Are you okay?"

I blink away the haze. "Pinch me."

His eyes narrow. "What?"

"Pinch me."

He raises an eyebrow as he gazes into my eyes, his finger still against my chin. "Is that your thing?"

"My thing?" I ask, more confused than ever.

"Your kink."

"No," I say quickly, mortified that he even thought that. "Pinch me so I know if I'm dreaming."

He smiles. "I'm not pinching you."

"If you want to kiss me again, Asher Gallo, you'll pinch me," I say in my sternest voice.

He slides his other hand against my bare leg, stopping right above my knee. My entire body comes alive, with goose bumps scattering everywhere from the lightness of his touch. The tips of his fingers press into my skin before twisting.

"Ouch," I snap, not even a little mad.

"You told me to," he says as he pulls his hand away, taking my goose bumps with him.

"I know." I smile, knowing this isn't a dream. The entire day wasn't a figment of my unconscious imagination.

We are here.

Asher is here.

He wants to kiss me.

The teenage girl who still lives inside my body is doing backflips, something I could never do in real life. She is celebrating the milestone.

"Why did I pinch you?"

"I wanted to make sure I was awake."

Asher's laugh is low and deep. "I can assure you, you're very much awake. And if I put you to sleep, I'm doing it wrong."

"Kiss me," I tell him, done with talking about thoughts that this was a delusion.

I don't have to tell him again, and I don't even prepare myself as Asher brings his face closer, lifting my chin higher, and takes my mouth like he's done it a million times before.

He doesn't kiss anything like other men I've kissed before. They were all dry lips and forcing their tongue into my mouth like they were searching for the secrets of the universe somewhere near my molars.

But not Asher.

Asher's kiss isn't forceful or rushed. It's soft yet demanding. Sensual yet hungry. His kiss is something people write poems about.

But before I have a chance to memorize everything about the moment, Asher pulls away. "We'll finish this when you come back."

I blink, trying to get my bearings. "What?"

"When you come back for school, we'll finish what we started."

It's sweet. Way sweeter than I ever imagined Asher being. But the boy I knew in high school isn't the man in front of me. And now's my chance. It's now or never. Things could change by fall for either of us, and I'm not willing to risk it.

"Fuck fall, Asher," I whisper, staring into his eyes.

It's his turn to blink. "What?" he whispers back, looking shocked and confused.

"I don't want to wait."

I've always been patient. I've always been the good girl. But that time is over. I'm an adult now. I don't need to fit into anyone's perfect mold except my own. I am entering a new area—finding pleasure in all aspects of my life. And right now, that includes banging Asher Gallo's brains out until he goes so stupid he can't form words.

Realization of what I said spreads across his face. "You don't want to wait?"

I shake my head, trying to control my breathing.

I've never wanted another man more than I do him in this moment.

"Well, fuck it. You don't have to tell me twice," he says and lunges forward, covering my body with his own.

I moan as he slides his hand under my kitten nightshirt and his mouth comes down over mine. His palm scorches my flesh, sending goose bumps scattering everywhere across my body.

I try not to think too much as Asher's tongue pushes against my lips, and I open for him, taking all he is willing to give. He tastes sweet, everything I always imagined he would when we were younger.

The way he kisses me doesn't disappoint either. It is soft and forceful at the same time, making my body feel like it is burning from the inside out. His hands skate across my bare flesh, exploring every inch he can get to easily.

My hands move to his shorts, palming his cock through the rough material. He is bigger than I thought he'd be. It is a nice surprise and kicks up my want for him to an even higher level.

I ache for him. Yearn for everything I always dreamed about when I was really too young to have those thoughts.

He moans into my mouth, sending the vibrations deep into my body. "I want you," he murmurs against my lips as his fingers trace the edge of my panties.

"Take me." I squeeze his dick harder. "I want you inside me, Asher."

He groans before he slides his hands into my panties and his fingertips find my clit. My back arches, the sensation almost overwhelming. I open my legs farther, giving him better access to every inch of me.

He pulls his mouth away, gliding his soft lips down the side of my neck. "You're dripping, baby," he says against my pulse.

"Stop talking." I push my middle forward, wanting and needing more. "Make me come."

I can almost feel Asher's smile against my neck. "Oli, I'm going to make you pass out."

He slides down my body, flipping up my kitten nightshirt as his knees hit the floor. His hands are at the waistband of my panties a second later, yanking them down my legs. "I want to taste you."

All I can do is watch in fascination, lifting my ass until my panties are off. Asher throws them across the room before he grabs my legs, pulling me to the edge of the couch until my bottom is hanging over the side.

"Lie back," he says softly, his eyes pinned on mine.

I do as I'm told, gripping anything I can to tether myself to in this moment. Asher Gallo's about to have his head buried in my…

My body nearly levitates as his mouth comes down on my clit, covering me in a warm heat. I melt into the cushions, trying not to hyperventilate at the reality of what's happening.

I've never been so forward when it comes to sex, but I've spent way too many nights dreaming of this moment. Since I ran into Asher at the grocery store, it's been the only thing on my mind.

If I left town and this all fell to shit, I'd kick myself in my own ass if I didn't at least have a few sexual experiences to add to the scrapbook in my brain.

Asher's tongue sweeps around my clit, circling at the perfect speed as he sucks me in. My eyes roll back on their own, unable to stop the pleasure from overtaking me.

"Right there," I mumble, or at least I think I do. I could be speaking in tongues, but it wouldn't matter to me as long as he keeps doing what he's doing.

Asher's fingers slide through my wetness before pushing inside, filling me. That's all it takes to send me closer to the edge.

My toes curl as the orgasm starts to build way too early. Damn Asher and his talented tongue. I wanted the feeling to last forever…or at least longer than my body allowed. It betrays me, sending the orgasm crashing over me like a tidal wave.

I want to moan his name, but there isn't any oxygen inside my lungs to make a sound. I could die in this moment, and I wouldn't care. The orgasm is that amazing.

Before I have a chance to open my eyes, Asher is on his feet, yanking his shorts down his legs.

I blink back the fuzziness, trying to focus on his nakedness.

"Fuck," I whisper as his body comes into focus and his shirt falls to the floor next to his shorts.

He smirks at me, not giving any shits about his nudity. "Well?" he motions down his body and then back up. "Everything you imagined?"

If he hadn't just had his head buried between my legs only a handful of seconds ago, I would blush. But it isn't in me. I've barely had a chance to catch my breath. "Yep," I say, letting my eyes linger a bit longer than necessary on his impressive member. "Not too bad. I can work with it."

His eyes flash before narrowing. "You can work with it?"

I shrug, my legs still wide open, pussy on full display. "Well, yeah."

Asher doesn't waste another moment as he stalks forward, grabs my legs, and slides right inside me like he was always meant to be there.

CHAPTER 7
ASHER

"SOMEONE GOT LUCKY," Gigi says as I walk into Inked the next afternoon with my legs wobbling like they're made out of jelly.

I narrow my gaze on her as I stalk by, already late setting up for my first client. "Zip it."

Gigi chuckles, smacking Lily on the arm. "Told you, bitch."

"Damn it. I thought Olive would put up a little bit of a fight," Lily tells her.

I take a few steps backward, stopping when I'm next to the counter where the two little gossips are sitting. "Watch what you say about Olive."

They share a look, one I've seen before. Before they burst into a fit of giggles.

Pike steps into the waiting room, shaking his head as he takes in the three of us. "Man, he's shot. S. H. O. T," he tells them, not having my back.

"I remember a time when you were pussy-whipped," I tell him, leaning one arm on the counter, knowing I'm not going to get much work done until we have the conversation.

Pike smiles and smacks me on the back. "Fuck. I still am, Ash. When it's the right one, you never go back to a time before."

"Fuck that," I tell him. "I'm stronger than you are."

All three of them laugh louder, and I grit my teeth, trying not to get upset with their bullshit.

"Ash, no man is strong when it comes to the magic spell the right pussy puts on you," Pike explains, but he makes absolutely no sense. "You'll see."

"Speak for yourself." I raise my chin, snarling a little.

The idea of being whipped doesn't aggravate me. I'd probably do just about anything for Olive right now. If I am honest with myself, I am already whipped. But that doesn't mean I won't argue about it with Pike and deny that simple fact for as long as I possibly can.

Rocco marches into Inked with an iced coffee in his hand, and his smile immediately falls the moment his gaze lands on the four of us. "What's up?"

Pike ticks his head toward me. "Dumbass here doesn't think he can be pussy-whipped. He said, and I quote, 'I'm stronger than you are.'"

Rocco snorts. "A dumbass indeed."

"Who's a dumbass?" Rebel asks when she comes barreling through the front door seconds after Rocco, juggling her phone in one hand, her purse hanging off her arm, and an even larger iced coffee in her other hand. "What did I miss?"

"Nothing," I snap.

Rebel's eyes swing my way. "Aww. You got lucky with Olive. I'm so happy for you."

What in the actual hell? Do I have a neon sign above my head to alert my entire nosy family about my sexual exploits?

"Everyone needs to stop," I tell them, letting my gaze move around the room to each of them. "What happened between Olive and me stays between us, and it's none of your business."

"When have we ever kept secrets?" Gigi asks.

"It's called privacy," I explain.

"There's no such thing in this family. You know this," Rocco says.

I suck in a deep breath, wishing they'd stop but knowing they never will. "We're done here," I tell them before stalking into the back room to get my supplies.

"I'm so happy for him," Lily says to the assholes I left in the front of the shop.

"He deserves happiness," Gigi says.

I smile to myself as I grab the extra supplies out

of the cabinet. I love my cousins, even when they want to know way too much information.

"It's time for him to settle down. He's the last one," Rebel says.

I've worn that title as a badge of honor ever since Stone found Opal. I am the last holdout, and I wasn't looking to find someone anytime soon. But that changed when Olive showed up out of nowhere.

My phone beeps before I leave the storage room, and I fish it out of my back pocket, needing an escape.

> Olive: I had a good time last night. If it's nothing more than that, thanks for the memories.

I stare at the screen, trying to decipher her words. First, it was more than good. It was fucking fantastic. I used all my best moves, and based on the way she moaned, good doesn't even begin to describe it. Second, we went over this…it is something more. Way more.

> Me: Babe…be honest. It was only good?

I shake my head as I stash my phone back in my pocket, pick up my tray of supplies, and head to my station.

"What's that look?" Stone asks as he scrolls through his favorite social media app on his phone.

I swear he hasn't looked up and would have no idea what the look was on my face, but maybe he has skills I never knew about. "What look?"

"Disbelief."

"Nothing," I mutter, not wanting to discuss what Olive and I did last night and how it wasn't even close to good… It was fucking unbelievable.

"Didn't get lucky, did you?"

I give Stone the middle finger as I sit down on my chair. "Dude, you know me."

Stone chuckles as he leans back, finally turning off the screen on his phone. "I do. That's why I said it."

"Fucker," I mumble under my breath. "Last night was great. Everything I hoped it would be and more."

A smile spreads across Stone's face. "When does she come back?"

I shrug and blow out a breath. "She said it could be a few months. School starts in the fall, but I think after last night, she'll find a reason to come back sooner."

He crosses his arms over his chest and raises a single eyebrow. "You think you're that good in bed?"

I nod. "You better believe it."

"Good morning," Tamara says, breezing into the customer waiting room and talking loudly enough to announce her presence to the entire shop.

"Fuck," I hiss, knowing she's here to be nosy. She could text or call like a normal person. No. Not my sister. My sister has to make it an event to put her nose where it doesn't belong when it comes to me.

"Tam," Gigi says, her voice filled with excitement. You'd think they haven't seen each other in forever by the way she greets her. "What the fuck are you doing here?"

"Came to check on my little brother."

I growl, wishing she'd stop reminding everyone I'm her "little" brother. I tower over Tamara and have been bigger than her since I was sixteen. She may be older, but I'm certainly larger.

"Oh, girl. He's soooooo whipped," Lily tells my sister.

"Like…" Gigi makes a whip sound. "Gone."

"You think she's the one?" Tamara asks them instead of me. "Because I do."

Like, what the fuck? Wouldn't you ask the actual person—meaning me—if they were in love? No. Not in my family. My family must gossip about a relationship status. I swear they believe they manifest the future with their bullshit.

"I do," Gigi says.

"Me too," Lily adds.

"Fuck yeah," Jo joins in with the girls.

Stone makes a face at me, waiting for me to confirm or deny their discussion. "She it?" he asks me.

I lift my arm and rub the back of my neck, suddenly feeling the heat and severity of the situation. "I don't know, man. I've never felt this way."

Stone tilts his head, studying me as he rubs the stubble on his jaw. "Like eternal doom and ridiculous excitement?"

I collapse backward against my chair, looking at him in disbelief. "Is that what love feels like?"

"It's the best and worst thing I've ever experienced or felt in my entire life."

I jerk my head back, confused as hell. "And you're happy about that?"

He nods with one corner of his mouth turned up. "I wouldn't change a damn thing."

"Fucking bananas," I mutter.

"I've never been happier."

"Then why is it the worst?"

He sighs. "Because if it all crumbles tomorrow, I'd be fucking wrecked."

"That won't happen."

He rubs a hand down the side of his face. "Not if I have anything to say about it, but weirder shit has happened."

"You won't fuck it up," I reassure him.

"But that's how you know you're in love. You can't imagine life without the other person in it. You barely remember a time before they came into your life."

"I'm not there…not yet," I admit. "But if there's anyone who can make me feel that way, it's Olive. She's just…"

"She had a glow-up, brother. A huge glow-up."

I tilt my head, scrunching my face. "Will I start talking like a chick when I fall in love? Because the Stone I knew, the one who was banging multiple bitches a night at the clubs, wouldn't use the words 'glow-up.'"

"You might, and if you call them bitches in front of Olive, Opal, or any of the women in this family, they're going to beat your ass to a bloody pulp."

"I'm not stupid. I wouldn't say that around them."

Stone's eyes move over my shoulder, and his eyebrows rise.

A knot forms in my stomach, and I don't need to turn around to know that Tamara's right behind me. I can only imagine her face. The shame. The anger. I hang my head, figuring it's time to start backpedaling and put the blame on Stone because my sister won't hurt him as much. "I only speak about women, all women, with respect. You should watch how you talk about them, Stone."

Stone lifts his hands. "I didn't say shit."

"So," Tamara says, her heels clicking against the tile floors, "what happened with Olive?"

The knot loosens only slightly because my sister is skilled at striking when you least expect it. "It went great," I tell her, keeping my body tight and waiting for the retaliation for the derogatory way I spoke about the opposite gender.

Tamara walks around me, plopping down on the

table in front of my chair. She fills my field of vision, wrapping her fingers around the edges of the table as she leans forward. "And?"

"We're talking."

"Talking about what?"

"The future."

Her eyes narrow. "You didn't lock that shit down?"

I blow out a breath at the ridiculousness of the question. "What does that even mean?"

"Did you take her off the market and let her know that she's the only one for you?"

"We just reunited, Tam. Give us a minute."

She shakes her head, making a tsking sound. "It only takes a minute for another man to steal your girl."

"Then she wasn't mine to begin with."

My sister rocks backward. "That's mighty grown up of you—and also very, very stupid."

"I told her how I feel, sis. I'm not an idiot."

She laughs. "That may be the funniest thing you've said in a long time."

"Stop," I warn her, hating that I have to rehash the topic of Olive over and over again with this group. "She'll be back, and we'll take it from there."

"You want her to be yours, you make sure that shit is locked down tight."

"Tight?" I ask her, wanting more clarification of

what's going to get her off my ass in the very near future.

She kicks her legs back and forth, barely missing my kneecaps with each pass. "Just make sure she doesn't feel like another notch on your bedpost."

"I would never do that."

Her lips flatten as she leans forward, her legs stopping, and gets right in my face. "You always do that. If you do it to her, I'm going to permanently alter your ability to have a child, using my favorite pair of black boots."

My balls ache at the very thought of being kicked by my sister. "I'll treat her right. I promise."

She leans a little closer, staring me straight in the eye. "And the next time I hear you refer to women as bitches, I am going to beat your ass to a bloody pulp."

I swallow, not bothering with a funny reply. My sister would beat the living hell out of me, and there's nothing I could do about it. I'd never hit her back. That shit stopped when we were kids. Hitting a woman, even my asshole sister, is never something I'd do. "Never again."

She smiles, staring at me a few more seconds before she backs away, straightening her spine. "Good. Smart guy."

"Now—" she hops off my table and smooths down the front of her shirt "—I have to get to the garage and have lunch with my husband."

"Aw, can't you stay longer?" I ask her, not meaning a damn word, and she knows it.

She extends a long, pointy finger in my direction. "Don't be a dick."

I shrug. "Only way I know how to be."

"Later, Stone," she calls out, not looking in his direction before her heels click against the floor and she's back out with the other ladies.

"She's intense," Stone whispers.

"You're fucking lucky you got sweet little Opal. Bastard."

"She's not always sweet," Stone argues. "Trust me."

"Does she ever come close to Tamara?"

Stone shakes his head and shivers. "No, thank fuck."

My ass vibrates, and I reach back, grabbing my phone, hoping it's a text reply from Olive.

Olive: It was a night I'll never forget.

Me: Baby, when you come back, I plan to relive it.

Olive: I look forward to you trying to outdo yourself.

Me: Trying? There's no trying to it. It'll happen.

Shit.

I'd used all my best moves, and she's hoping I can

outdo it. I need to do some studying, learn new skills and more creative ways to please her.

> Olive: I have to go. We're about to take off. Talk soon.

> Me: Safe travels.

And just like that…she's gone.

CHAPTER 8
OLIVE

THE TAP and Grind is the best coffee shop near campus. I spent hours upon hours here, ingesting an ungodly amount of caffeine when studying for finals.

It will be the place I'll miss most after my move back to Florida. I'm sure there're good indie coffee shops near campus or my house, but none of them will be as great as this place.

"Hey, Olive. Where did you disappear to?" Elliott, my favorite male barista, asks me as soon as I step up to the register.

I smile, loving that the staff here is friendly and gets to know the customers. "I went to check out my new school."

His eyes widen before his shoulders fall. "Damn. We hate to see you go."

"I know," I tell him, reaching inside my purse for my credit card. "I'll miss this place and all of you."

"Where you headed to?"

"Back to Florida where I grew up."

"At least you're staying in the sunshine and warmth."

"Yeah. I couldn't deal with the cold."

The woman behind me sighs, clearly annoyed with us chitchatting instead of making progress with my order.

"Anyway, I'll take the usual."

"Quad upside down with oat milk, five pumps of sugar-free vanilla, and two pumps of brown sugar."

I nod. "Can I have some chocolate foam on top too?"

"Anything for my girl."

My cheeks instantly heat. In another time, I totally could've hooked up with Elliott. He's easy on the eyes and kind, but our timing had been off. By the time I met him, I was already with Chris, which turned out to be a horrible mistake.

"Thanks, Elliott."

He leans over as I jam my credit card into the reader. "You want to catch a drink before you blow town?"

By a drink, I think he's asking if I want to hook up, and while the offer would've been tempting a few weeks ago, I can't do that now. My heart's somewhere else, with someone else. "I wish I could, Elliott, but I can't. It's really sweet of you to ask, though."

He gives me a chin lift. "No worries. Maybe if you ever come back to visit."

I smile at him, knowing it'll never happen. "For sure."

"Will you be back in before you go?"

"Yes. I don't leave for a while. School doesn't start until fall."

"Good," he says.

"Excuse me," the woman behind me says, and I turn to look at her. "I'm in kind of a hurry. I'm going to be late to my summer class, and the teacher is a beast."

"Sorry," I say, stepping to the side and then sliding down the counter to the pickup area. I shove my phone and credit card into my purse, wanting to spend time people watching, something I didn't get to do when my nose was stuck in a book.

I feel a tap on my shoulder, and I turn around. My stomach instantly knots the moment my gaze lands on the man I didn't ever want to see again.

"Hi," Chris says softly, tucking his hands into the front pockets of his jeans. "I'm glad I ran into you."

I cross my arms over my chest, trying to swallow down the bitter taste on my tongue. "Did you run into me, or have you been waiting for me?"

He looks around, not meeting my eyes. "I had to see you."

"No, you didn't. We have nothing to say to each other."

People move around us, oblivious to our history together. I wish I were clueless too. The memory of that night is burned on my retinas, and I'm not sure if I'll ever be able to get rid of it. I'm over the hurt part of our relationship ending, but the betrayal is harder to get past.

He pulls a hand from his pocket and reaches out to touch my arm, but I pull away. "No," I snap.

He yanks his hand back like the air itself burns him. "Sorry."

I tilt my head, glaring at him. "Are you?"

His Adam's apple bobs before he gazes down at the brown tile. "I am," he whispers.

"Olive," the new female barista calls out and places my quad on the counter.

I grab my coffee, but before I can take a sip, Chris reaches out and touches the back of my arm. I whip around, careful not to spill a drop, and growl at Chris. I lean forward, getting into his space, which doesn't seem to faze him. "If you ever touch me, you'll lose those fingers. Do. You. Understand?"

Chris's face loses all color. "Olive, please," he begs. "I need to explain."

"No." I shake my head, my hair swishing from side to side. "You don't, and I don't want to hear a damn thing either. There are no excuses for what you did, and we're over. There's nothing more to discuss."

He squares his shoulders, standing a little taller. "I think I deserve a chance to explain."

I cackle at the absurdity. "You don't deserve shit, Chris. Your dick didn't just fall into her. You made that damn choice, and now I'm making mine. You don't deserve my time to explain. I don't deserve to have to hear your bullshit either. I wasted enough of my life on a worthless piece of shit like you. Stay the fuck away from me."

The coffee shop becomes a little quieter, the customers overhearing our conversation and eager to hear more.

"You're making a scene," Chris tells me, making this interaction my fault.

If I weren't so exhausted and in need of caffeine, I would've thrown my coffee right in his face. "You're the one who won't leave me be, Chris. We're done here. Forget I exist." I hold my head high and start to walk away.

"You're nothing but a stuck-up bitch," Chris says loud enough for everyone in the coffee shop to hear.

I don't falter in my stride, marching out of the shop and right into the rain. Maybe Mother Nature can wash the dirt of that entire conversation off me. Chris is no one to me. He's not worth the anger that wants to take root deep in my belly.

Next door to the coffee shop is a great little bookstore and the perfect escape from Chris in case he's not done being an asshole. As soon as I make it to the paranormal section, my phone rings.

"Hey," I say, slinking down on the floor, resting my back against the shelves.

"Hey, beautiful," Asher says, his voice instantly making all the bullshit I just went through with Chris vanish. "What's up? What are you doing?"

"I'm at the bookstore with my favorite cup of coffee."

"Only a cup?"

I laugh. "A quad."

"Damn. That's a lot of caffeine."

"It's my morning drink."

"You're going to have more than that?"

"Maybe," I say, smiling.

"What's up today?"

I sigh, pushing my head against the books. "Not too much. Classes are over. I'm probably going to start packing."

"Coming early?"

Ever since I left Tampa, I haven't been able to think about anything else except Asher and all the possibilities.

"There's nothing for me to stay for here."

Originally, I'd planned to leave closer to the start of school, but that was because I didn't want to leave Chris any earlier than I had to. But now, I have no reason to stick around. I certainly don't want a repeat of today's Chris interaction.

"That stung a little."

"Sorry," I tell him, shaking my head. "I didn't mean it like that."

"You're coming for me, aren't you? You can admit it."

A woman walks by, staring at me with her lip curled. She obviously doesn't like that I'm sitting on the floor, talking on the phone in a bookstore, but I couldn't care less. After what just happened in the coffee shop, I need a moment to unwind and remember there are still good guys in this world.

"What do I get if I say yes?" I ask him, ignoring the woman and her dirty looks.

"Orgasms…a lot of orgasms."

I bite my lip as my body tingles, remembering the way he made me feel when he worshipped my body. "You're mighty sure of yourself," I tease him.

"Baby girl, I know all the ways to make your toes curl."

My belly does a weird flip at the smoothness of his voice and the words he speaks. "Shh. I'm in public."

"Are you blushing?"

I touch my cheeks, feeling the warmth underneath my fingertips. "A little."

I bow my head, hiding my face from strangers. Could they tell we were talking naughty to each other by simply looking at my face? It feels like it.

"Too bad," he mutters. "I thought we could video chat and get a little dirty."

"I don't… I can't…"

"Ever done it?"

"No," I whisper.

"Do you want to?"

His voice makes me want to chant yes and tear off my clothes, but my brain is slamming on the brakes and bringing me right back to reality.

"I don't know. I'd rather wait until we see each other again." I stare up at the stack of books in front of me, picturing Asher naked.

His body is a work of art. Sculpted hard lines everywhere and covered in ink. Pure perfection.

"Wait for an orgasm?"

I shrug even though he can't see.

"Words, Olive," he says softly.

"I don't know. Maybe. But I'm not comfortable doing stuff—" I glance around, making sure no one's in earshot "—through video chat. It's something I've never done before."

I hear a low rumble on the other end. "Save yourself for me. No orgasms until I get to give you one. Got me?"

"But what if I…"

"No. No touching yourself. Do you think you can do that?"

"I don't know."

"Be a good girl and try for me."

"I will," I whisper like the people around me can hear what Asher's saying on the other end of the phone. "You do the same."

He gasps. "You don't want me to touch myself?"

"No orgasms until we see each other."

He growls. "Do you know how hard that is for a guy?"

"It won't kill you, Asher."

"It may."

He's so dramatic. All men are when it comes to orgasms. I swear it's more important to them than anything in the world, including food.

"You better be coming here early because I'm not waiting months to come, Oli."

"I'm making my plans to be there much earlier."

"How early is much earlier?"

"A few weeks."

He repeatedly breathes deeply like he's about to hyperventilate. "Weeks is a long time to hold out."

"You can do it, Ash. I have faith in you. Mind over matter. Just try not to think about my tits too much," I tease him, knowing I'm playing dirty.

"Fucking hell," he mutters, followed by a slew of curse words he mumbles under his breath.

"I got to go. Talk soon."

"Later, baby girl."

And as soon as I disconnect the call, the air feels lighter, and everything that happened earlier doesn't even matter. It's as if it never existed.

CHAPTER 9
ASHER

I LEAN BACK into the couch cushion, spent from the late-night session working on a large back piece.

"What's wrong?" Gramps asks as he sits down next to me to watch the game before dinner.

"I'm just tired."

He chuckles as he slaps my knee. "You don't even know what tired is, kid."

I stare at his face full of deep lines, showing his years. He's still handsome, looking younger than he really is. I hope when I'm his age, I look as good as him.

"I know, Gramps. It was just a late night."

"Yeah?" His eyes sparkle with a flash of excitement. "Anything fun?"

I shake my head. "My client's back piece took longer than I expected. He needed a lot of breaks because he couldn't handle the pain."

"Pansy," Gramps whispers as he turns his focus to the television.

I laugh. "No truer words."

"Is business good?" he asks, but his attention isn't on me, and I'm not even sure he cares about the answer.

"Busier than ever."

"Good. Good."

Tamara sits on the armrest next to me, bumping me with her shoulder. "What's new, little brother? How's Olive?"

"Olive?" Gramps asks, his gaze shifting my way. "Who's Olive?"

"A girl, Gramps," Tamara answers for me, always loving to stir the pot, and she knows my grandparents are chomping at the bit for their last grandchild to get hitched. "A beautiful, smart girl."

"Does Gram know?" he asks her, ignoring me entirely.

"There's nothing to know," I tell him, hoping to put an end to the conversation.

"Not yet," Tamara says, "but she's moving here soon, and she had the biggest crush on Asher when he was young."

"Really?" he asks, eager to hear the answer.

"They ran into each other not too long ago, and as soon as I saw them together, I knew Asher was a goner."

"What are you talking about?" Uncle Joe asks as he sits in the recliner on the other side of the room.

"We're talking about Asher's girlfriend," Gramps answers, throwing me right under the bus.

"Really?" Uncle Joe's facial expression matches my grandfather's from only moments ago. "Do we know her?"

"Olive Thornberry," Tamara says.

Uncle Joe's eyebrows furrow. "The name sounds familiar, but I can't place her."

"Her family moved away a long time ago. She has an older brother named River."

"Right." Uncle Joe nods as his face softens. "River was a little asshole, but his sister was a quiet, sweet thing."

"I'm sure he's still an asshole," I mutter, giving up on moving the conversation away from Olive.

"Are you thinking about hanging up your hat?" Uncle Joe asks.

"What hat?" Gramps asks, staring up at the top of my head with his brow pulled in.

"He's not talking about a hat, hat, Gramps."

"Being a player…playing the field," Uncle Joe explains. "You ready to settle down?"

I hold out my hands. "Whoa. We're barely dating. I haven't thought much beyond that."

"Barely dating?" Uncle Joe asks with a raised eyebrow.

I nod.

"You've never even barely dated."

"I have too."

He raises that eyebrow higher. "Liar."

I rub my hand across my chin, hating discussing my feelings and relationships. "I don't know what Olive and I are or aren't yet."

"Don't listen to him." Tamara smacks my shoulder with the back of her hand. "They're going to get married."

I narrow my eyes as I turn my gaze toward her. "Geez, Tam. Can you let us date for a bit before you have us walking down the aisle?"

"Oh, they're totally getting married," Lily says, striding into the family room with a glass of wine. "A girl can tell, and every single woman in this family thinks it'll happen."

I roll my eyes. "You're all bananas."

Lily shakes her head, smiling at me over the rim of her glass. "Thou doth protest too much."

I sigh. "Whatever."

"Are we talking about Olive?" Gigi asks as she sits down next to her father's legs on the floor. "I've been waiting to talk about her."

"It's all you people talk about anymore." I cross my arms over my chest, wishing I could get up and stalk off, but that would only make things worse.

"Are we talking about Olive?" Mammoth stands behind Tamara, placing his hands on her shoulders.

"Yeah, baby," she says, peering up at him over her

shoulder. "Asher's in denial about what's going to happen."

"It's hard for a man to close one chapter and open another. We're not as adventurous when it comes to our feelings," Mammoth explains like he speaks for everyone with a dick and balls.

"It's not hard." I rest my elbow on the armrest next to Tamara's hip, placing my cheek in my palm. "It's not that big of a deal."

Tamara chuckles, quickly joined by the other women who are near us.

"Are you delusional or unwilling to admit how you really think or feel?" Tamara asks, crossing her arms over her chest, and she stares down at me with a look my mother gave me a million times when I was younger.

"Be nice to your brother," Ma says as she comes into the family room.

"Thanks, Ma," I say, knowing she'll always have my back.

"He's going through his bitch phase, but that doesn't mean we can't be supportive."

"Hey!" I shake my head. "I am not."

Ma leans over, stroking my cheek with the back of her hand. "It's all right. You're going through some scary things right now, but it'll all be okay."

"You're all delusional," I say to her, but I'm speaking to everyone. "We barely know each other."

"I knew I wanted to marry your mom the

moment I laid eyes on her," Pop says, pouring gasoline onto the fire. "When you know, you know."

"I was crazy about your gram. Man, she was a looker…still is." Gramps twists his back to get a clear line of sight into the kitchen. "When I saw her, I knew no other woman would do."

"You feel that way too?" I ask Mammoth as he positions himself behind my sister like he's standing guard over her.

"I was too busy trying to keep her ass alive to think much about anything else."

"He's lying," she says, touching his hand as it rests on her shoulder. "He knew."

"Princess, you weren't even there to see me."

"I didn't know you existed, but the moment our eyes locked… Bam!" She smacks the back of one hand into her other palm. "It was over for him."

"Whatever she says," Mammoth answers, dipping his chin at my sister.

"Give that boy some time to process things," Aunt Izzy says as she wades into the conversation from the kitchen behind us. "He's young, and he wants to be sure. We don't even know this girl. She could be trouble and a heartbreaker."

Rosie snorts. "Olive is the furthest thing from trouble, Auntie. She was too busy studying to do anything bad. If there was a picture of a bookworm in the dictionary, it would be of Olive with her black-rimmed glasses."

"Aww," Aunt Izzy sings, "Asher deserves a good girl."

Tamara drops her chin, staring at my aunt with furrowed brows. "Does he, though?"

Aunt Izzy nods. "He's a good kid."

Tamara cackles. "That's some bullshit," she says under her breath.

"Can we talk about something else, please?" I beg.

Gramps lifts his arm, placing his heavy hand on my shoulder. "I got my prostate exam this week," he says with a squeeze of my shoulder. "Better?"

I wince at the same time everyone else does. "I don't even know what that entails, but I know it's not good."

"See?" he says, smiling at me. "There's worse topics we can talk about."

I tilt my head, wishing I could slink away. "Maybe I should go help in the kitchen," I start to stand, but my gramps pushes on my shoulder, forcing me back down.

"I want my dinner to be edible," he says. "New topic…Christmas."

"What about it?" Uncle Joe leans forward, placing his elbows on his knees. "It's in December."

"Thanks, smartass." Gramps waves off my uncle and continues. "I think we should do a family trip this Christmas instead of gifts."

"I could use a trip to the Bahamas," Aunt Izzy says.

"No," Gramps says, shaking his head. "I'm thinking some place more Christmasy."

Aunt Izzy places her hands on her hips, dropping a shoulder full of attitude. "More Christmasy? What's more Christmasy than aqua water and calming ocean waves?"

"The mountains and snow."

A unilateral groan comes from everyone in the room.

Grandpa stands and adjusts his pants, ready to make his case. "Listen, I'm older than dirt and I don't know how many more Christmases I have left on this earth, and I want to see snow again. I want to sit around a fireplace with my kids, grandkids, and great-grandkids and sing carols before I die."

"Sweet Jesus," Aunt Izzy mutters. "Way to lay on the guilt, Pops."

"You're not older than dirt," Uncle Joe adds. "You have a lot of Christmases left."

Gramps stares at my uncle. "How many?"

Uncle Joe shrugs. "Fuck if I know."

"Exactly. I already booked the cabin."

"How in the hell are we all going to fit into a cabin, Pop?" Aunt Izzy asks.

Gramps smiles so damn big. The old man is proud of himself. If he wants us to go to the moon for Christmas, I'd be right there with him. I may not be overly excited about freezing my ass off, but hitting the slopes for the first time sounds like a good way to spend the holiday.

"It's more like a mansion than a cabin. It's big enough for everyone. No one's going to be sleeping in a tent. There's even a heated indoor pool."

"Sold," Ma says, raising a hand. "But is there a hot tub?"

"Yes," he says.

"Fabulous," Ma replies. "We'll do whatever you want, Dad. It's your Christmas as much as ours, and we'll go anywhere you want and be happy as long we're all together." She looks around when she says that, telling every person in the room not to pull any shit.

"Should we invite Chicago?" Gramps asks everyone.

"Is there room?" Aunt Fran, Gramps's sister, asks from the kitchen. How she even heard the conversation, I'll never know. The woman could hear a pin drop from a thousand feet away. She's scary sometimes. "I'd love for Santino and the kids to come."

"There's a cabin next door," he tells her. "It was still available the last time I checked."

"Grab it. I'll treat them," Fran answers. "If they can't make it, it'll mean more room for us."

"I'll grab the cabin," Morgan, Fran's son and my first cousin, says. "We want to come too."

"I had you included with us, Morgan. You're

every bit a part of this family as anyone else," Gramps says to him.

Morgan smiles. "Thanks, Uncle Sal."

Gramps gives him a chin lift. "Then it's settled. The whole gang will be there."

"Do you think Santino will come with the kids?" Fran asks.

"It's a free vacation. That cheap bastard will crawl through glass to get his ass there if it's free."

Uncle Joe laughs. "The man never likes to part with his money, but I'd ask Aunt Betty first. They may be on the outs again. Those two are like oil and water."

"Whether they come or not, we're headed north for Christmas," Gramps announces, looking like the Cubs just won the World Series.

CHAPTER 10
OLIVE

"HELLO." I don't bother looking, too busy shoving my clothes into the dryer before they fall onto the floor.

"Hey." Asher's voice comes through the speaker sounding smooth as silk.

Damn.

I try to keep my balance, using my knee to push in the last pieces while keeping the phone on my shoulder. "Hey yourself."

"What are you doing? You're out of breath."

"Laundry."

"It sounds a little more strenuous."

"I do big loads."

I do big loads? What's wrong with me? That sounded so…

"Well, okay," he breathes out.

"I hate laundry. The fewer loads I have to do, the better."

I hear a small bit of laughter on the other end of the phone. "When are you getting here?"

"I'll leave tomorrow afternoon, and then it's a two-day drive. So, before the weekend, if I make good time and don't hit any hiccups."

"Who's driving with you?"

I slam the dryer door a little too hard and wince, but Asher doesn't seem to notice the loud noise. "No one."

A rustling comes from his end. "Wait."

"What?" I ask, grabbing my phone from my shoulder and tapping the speaker button.

"You're driving alone?" His voice carries an air of disbelief like it's the most absurd thing in the world.

"Of course. I'm an adult." It won't be the first time I've done a long road trip by myself. "It's not that long of a drive."

"It's too far to do alone, Olive."

"Who says?" I stalk into my small galley-style kitchen, turning on the faucet to let the water turn cold and set my phone down on the counter next to the sink.

"Me."

I chuckle, shaking my head as I reach for a double-walled glass that doesn't let the ice melt as quickly as other glasses. "Well, it's a good thing you're not in charge of my life."

"What about River?" he says.

I press my glass against the ice maker that's built into my fridge and is on its last leg. I let his words fester as I slide over to the sink. "What about him?" I hold the cup underneath the faucet, wishing I could stick my head under instead. I'm unbelievably hot, and the heat wave raging outside isn't helping matters.

"He should be driving you."

I twist the faucet, cutting off the water, dumbfounded by his reply. "He's not my dad or my keeper, Asher. This isn't the 1950s."

"I know that, and it's way more dangerous than the fifties too. A woman—"

"Hold up," I snap, totally annoyed with him. "It doesn't matter what I have between my legs, Asher. I can drive myself across a few states and make it there alive."

"Just because you can doesn't mean you should."

I lift the tumbler to my lips, gulping down the water, trying to cool my insides along with my temper. Asher makes it seem like I'm not able to do something as simple as drive by myself because I have a vagina.

"Hello?" he says when I don't answer.

I take a deep breath once I've downed half the glass. "I'm here."

"Well?"

"Well, what?" I ask with an edge to my voice.

"Something could happen."

“I could get hit by a bus going to the grocery store tomorrow.”

“That’s not the same.”

“It is,” I argue.

He sighs. “Where are you going to stay along the way?”

“I’ll catch a few hours at a rest stop.”

There’s a low rumble of curse words on the other end of the line. “Are you fucking with me?”

I stare out the window at my dead grass, the heat killing off the last bits that my landlord didn’t bother to replace. “Why would I do that? I’m not fucking with you, Asher.”

He growls before he replies. “Do you know how unsafe that is?”

I glance up toward the ceiling, cursing under my breath now. “I’ve done it before and never felt unsafe, but I’m sure you’re going to explain all the ways I could die.”

I cross my arms over my chest and think about walking away from the phone, letting him talk to himself. “There’s more to fear than death.”

I grit my teeth, extending my arm out to hover my finger over the end button.

“Do not hang up on me.”

I blink, yanking my hand back like he has a camera on me. “I don’t need a lecture.”

“You’re not going alone.”

“I am.”

"You aren't."

"I am," I tell him, thrusting my phone out and disconnecting the call before he has a chance to continue the argument.

I immediately switch off the ringer, knowing damn well he's going to call back.

For the last month, we've talked every day on the phone, sometimes for hours. He's begged me to come back to Tampa early to spend time with him before starting school. Every conversation has been flirty and fun, but this one…this one leaves a bitter taste in my mouth.

I stare at the screen, watching as call after call comes in, but I hold fast, not answering a single one of them.

But the celebration is short-lived because he follows the calls with text messages. I can't stop myself from watching as each one rolls in.

Asher: I only want what's best for you.

Asher: Don't be mad at me.

Asher: I know you're grown.

But does he, though? Nothing about our conversation made it seem like he thought I was capable of taking care of myself. I've been on my own for years. No one has ever second-guessed my decisions, whether it was about travel or anything else.

Asher: I just want you safe.

Under any other circumstances, I would've already caved and called him back, but I need to dig my heels in now so we don't have this problem again in the future…if there is a future.

In all our talks, Asher has seemed to be devoted and said he wanted to try at a real relationship. But I know him and so do all my old friends who still live in the same town as him.

I've called a few, casually mentioning that I'd run into him. I wanted to hear what they had to say. Asher is liked. He has that kind of personality, but he is known as a player. That hasn't changed since high school.

Men make promises all the time, and they break them too. I don't really know what kind of man Asher is now besides his affinity for helping his grandmother and how much importance he places on his family.

My phone lights up again, but this time, it's my mom. "Hi, Mom," I say, trying to sound way more cheerful than I'm feeling. "What's up?"

"All packed up?" she asks.

"I am. Just a few more things to do before I can get on the road."

"That's nice, honey. Do you have enough money?"

See? My mother isn't the least bit concerned

about my driving cross-country except that I may not have enough money in my pocket to pay for gas.

"Yes, Mom. I'm going to the bank tomorrow to get cash, and I have my credit cards. I'll be fine."

"Great. Pull over if you get tired."

"I will."

"Call if you need anything."

"Okay."

"Love you."

"Love you too."

She doesn't even say goodbye before ending the call. That's been the extent of our interactions for the last few years. I won't hear from her again for about a week. I could go missing and be shipped to another country, and she wouldn't have a clue.

I don't even have a chance to put my phone down before it rings again. But this time, it's my brother.

"Hey," he says before I can say a word.

"Hey, Riv. What's up?"

"Why in the hell is Asher blowing up my phone?"

"What?" I screech, unable to control the tone of my voice. "You're kidding me."

"Nope," he clips. "He's called a few times and is texting me nonsense about your safety. Is there something I should know?"

I rest my ass against the countertop, leaning back in disbelief. "Fuck," I hiss, closing my eyes. "He's ridiculous."

"What's his problem?"

I sigh, letting my shoulders sag forward. "He's worried."

"About?"

"That I'll be murdered on my trip," I say softly.

River makes a hmphing sound. "It's possible, but unlikely."

My brother is always a ray of positivity, doing absolutely nothing to alleviate any anxiety I have about the trip.

"I'll be fine," I tell him, but I know he's not worried, just like my parents aren't either.

"I know. You've done the drive a dozen times."

"And I'm still alive and breathing."

"Sure enough," he says and clears his throat. "Now, what are you going to do about Asher? I thought we had a talk about him."

"You talked. I listened."

Beyond that, there's nothing. My brother has no business sticking his nose into my personal life, especially my sexual activity. I've never given him shit for his lack of commitment when it comes to women.

"And none of it stuck, huh? In one ear and out the other?" he asks.

"People change, River. He's different."

"Men don't change that easily, Oli. Once a player, always a player."

I hate hearing him say those words. I know the likelihood that he is right is extremely high. I haven't found anyone who had said otherwise about Asher either.

"We're just having fun. Totally casual."

"I remember how you felt about him when we were young."

"I'm not that dumb girl anymore."

"You were never dumb, Oli. But you had a serious crush on him. I just want to make sure you…"

"River," I warn.

"Okay. Okay."

"Have I ever lectured you on your relationships?"

"No." He blows out a breath. "I'll butt out."

"Good."

"Impossible," he mutters. "Text me before you hit the road and when you get there. It's good if someone knows what you're doing."

"I will," I promise him. "I have to go. I have a million things to do."

"Talk soon," he says.

"Yeah. Soon," I tell him, ending the call.

I need to spend the rest of the night packing up the odds and ends to take to the local charity drop-off tomorrow, but between my brother and Asher, I don't have the energy.

Instead, I drop down onto my couch and turn on the television, letting myself get lost in a reality television show about an over-the-top matchmaker.

I can't imagine putting my future into the hands of another. Meeting someone for a brief time and then getting married without truly knowing them? It boggles my mind.

I binge episode after episode, knowing this is the last time I'm going to be able to relax for a while. I'll be too busy moving in to my new place with a to-do list a mile long to get ready for grad school.

And before long, my eyes close, and I let my body sink deeper into the cushion as sleep takes me.

CHAPTER 11
ASHER

"SAY THAT AGAIN," Gigi says as I rush through the crowd of people to make my way outside.

"I need you to cancel all my appointments for the rest of the week. Move them around to whenever next week."

"Why?"

I raise my hand as soon as I see a cab coming my way. "I'm in Texas."

"What in the actual fuck, Asher? You were here yesterday and said nothing about Texas."

"I know. It wasn't a planned trip. Last-minute shit," I tell her as the cab stops in front of me, and I open the door. "I'll be back by the weekend, though."

"What's in Texas? What's the emergency?"

"Olive was going to drive to Florida alone. I'm fixing that."

I hear silence on the other end as I slide into the

back seat, handing the driver a tiny slip of paper with Olive's address written on it.

"Does she know you're coming?"

"No."

More silence.

"Does she want you to drive with her?"

"No."

The silence only gets louder.

"You're so fucked, cousin."

"I am not," I say, dropping my backpack between my feet on the surprisingly clean floor.

"She's going to be so pissed."

"You don't know that."

But I do know that, and Gigi is right. Olive is going to throw a fit that I booked a ticket, flew halfway across the country, and will be doing the drive with her even though she told me she could do it on her own. It just didn't sit right with me. If I have the ability and the means, which I do on both accounts, I can't sit idly by with my thumb up my ass, waiting for her to get to Tampa.

"I'd rather beg for forgiveness than ask for permission, Gigi."

My cousin sighs. "It's sweet but screwed up too. You're going to be doing a lot of begging. I mean, *a lot*, a lot."

"Whatever. I don't care if I have to beg for years as long as she's safe."

"Man, I wish I could be there when she opens the

door and sees your face. You might end up with a black eye."

I chuckle at the imagery of Olive trying to punch me. "Olive's not like that. She's a lady."

Gigi makes a tsking sound, and I know she's shaking her head, thinking about how stupid I am. "You're truly dumber than you look."

"I take offense to that," I tell her, watching as the cab driver weaves in and out of traffic like a man possessed.

"Of course you would," she mumbles.

"What's wrong?" Lily says in the background.

"Asher decided to fly to Texas to drive back with Olive so she wouldn't have to do it alone," Gigi explains to Lily.

"That's so sweet," Lily tells her.

"But Olive doesn't know and doesn't want his help."

Lily hisses. "He's about to be in some real shit."

"Yep," Gigi snaps. "I tried telling him, but he won't listen."

"His penis makes it impossible for words to penetrate his brain sometimes."

They chuckle in unison.

"You two suck," I tell them, rubbing the sleep from my eyes.

I caught the first flight in the morning, which was way before sunrise. That put me on the ground during morning rush hour, but based on GPS, Olive doesn't live more than fifteen minutes away from the airport.

I'll be there in plenty of time before she hits the road. She'll have no other option than to let me hitch a ride back with her. We can make it fun too. I've always liked road trips, and there's no better way to catch up with someone than to be stuck in a car with them for hours.

"She's going to be big mad. Big," Lily adds in the background. "I can't wait to see how it turns out, though."

"He's screwed, yeah?" Gigi asks her, having an entire conversation without me.

"Yep, and not in the way he's hoping," Lily says.

"She'll be fine," I tell them, hoping I'm right because there's no going back now.

"Keep us in the loop. If we don't hear from you tonight, we'll know she killed you and hid the body."

I give a mocking laugh. "You two are so dramatic. She's going to jump into my arms as soon as she sees my face."

They laugh again, but this time louder.

"Good luck, Ash. It was nice having you as a cousin," Gigi says to me.

"I'm done with this conversation." I disconnect the call as soon as they start laughing again. "Assholes," I mumble.

Me: Good morning, sunshine.

Olive hasn't replied to me since last night. It's early, though, and maybe she's still asleep. I stare at the screen, waiting for any signs of life. My heart leaps as soon as I see the three dots on the screen.

Olive: Hey.

Asher: Sorry about last night.

Olive: Me too.

I breathe a sigh of relief. She's not mad at me anymore. My cousins can choke on their words. Olive is, in fact, going to leap into my arms as soon as she sees me. Everyone likes a surprise, especially when it's me.

Me: What time are you leaving?

Olive: In about an hour.

Shit. I am just barely going to make it. If my flight had been any later, I would've been screwed.

Me: Earlier than you planned?

Olive: I want to get ahead of some storms. I hate driving in a downpour.

Me: Me too.

I close our text message and open up my group chat with my family.

Me: She's not mad at me anymore.

Gigi: Has she seen you?

Me: No.

Tamara: What's going on?

Oh boy. Here we go. My sister's going to have some bullshit to say, and they're all about to gang up on me…at least, the women will. The men will understand where I'm coming from. They'd do the same for their women.

Wait. Is Olive mine? Completely mine? I want her to be. I feel like it's right. I said that in so many words before she went back home, but I don't think she believed a word of it.

We had more than one conversation about it, actually. All of them ended weirdly, like Olive still didn't believe me.

But I'll make her understand and believe every word that comes out of my mouth when it comes to us as a couple.

I know good girls, and hell, I know bad ones too. While the bad ones can be fun, I've run out of patience with them. I want the good. I want Olive. I want to move on, grow up, start a family. None of that will be possible with anyone other than a good girl, and no one had captured my attention like Olive.

She caught it in high school, but I wasn't in the

right place for a girl like her. I would've ruined her forever.

Gigi: Your dumbass brother flew to Texas to drive back with Olive, but she doesn't know he's coming and doesn't want any help.

Tamara: Wait. What?

Me: She can't do the drive alone.

Tamara: Why?

Me: She's a woman.

I wince as soon as I send the message, knowing my sister will want to beat my ass for saying such a thing.

Tamara: You did not just say that.

Mammoth: Oh boy. He fucked up.

Pike: Big time.

Nick: Damn, dude. You don't say that shit out loud.

Me: Well, it's the truth.

Gigi: She's going to sock him right in the face when she opens the door and sees him standing there.

Tamara: She can blacken one eye, and I'll get the other for him uttering such completely misogynistic bullshit.

Luna: Can you take a video when she opens the door? I want to see her face.

Rosie: I'd pay big money to see that video.

Me: Shut up. It'll be good. She'll be happy.

Rebel: How are men so clueless?

Carmello: Hey now. We aren't.

Lily: They're clueless about being clueless.

Me: You're all going to eat your words when you see how happy she is.

Gigi: Bahaha. Moron.

Tamara: He didn't get the brains in the family.

Stone: Good luck, man. You got this.

Shit. If Stone thinks I've got it, I most certainly don't. I know the man got lucky with Opal, but being able to get into a woman's mind has never been his forte. He was always better at getting into their pants.

Me: See you all this weekend. I'm out.

Tamara: Out of his mind.

I close the chat window, turning off my notifications for the group text. I assume they'll be going on for hours about what an idiot I am, and I don't need to see that as I fight for my romantic life with Olive.

The cab pulls to the side of the road, and I look out over a large patch of dead grass to a small house. "We're here, sir. That'll be thirty dollars."

I reach into my back pocket and dig two twenties out of my wallet before handing them to the man. "Keep the change."

He smiles as he reaches over his shoulder, taking the money from my hand. "Good luck," he tells me as he ticks his head toward the door. "Want me to wait?"

"No. I've got this," I tell him, and he raises his eyebrows like he doesn't believe me.

Is anyone on my side?

I climb out of the cab and take a minute on the sidewalk to soak in the miserable sight of her place. It's not that it's not nice. It's just not as green as I thought it would be. It's nowhere near as lush and tropical as Florida.

Olive's small SUV is in the driveway, boxes filling the entire back seat and trunk area. At least she's ready to hit the road. I haven't seen but a few miles of Texas, but it's enough for me to know I don't need to see any more.

I stand tall, shoulders back, chin up, and march toward her front door with every bit of confidence I can muster.

I honestly don't care if she gets mad or not. I

won't and can't let her drive across multiple states by herself. She can't stay pissed at me forever, right?

The house has a yellow door, a bright pop of color, surrounded by the dreariest gray I've ever seen on an exterior. The yellow fits Olive, but the gray certainly does not.

"You've got this," I tell myself, stepping up to the door before taking a deep breath. "She's going to be happy."

I lift my hand and knock, bracing myself for whatever comes next.

CHAPTER 12
OLIVE

"LET ME CALL YOU BACK," I tell River as someone knocks on my door. "Someone's here."

"Text me before you get on the road."

"I will."

"Bye, sis."

I'm already behind, and the day has barely begun. I rush to the door, hoping one of my chatty neighbors isn't on the other side.

"Later," I tell him before tossing my phone onto the last pile of boxes left inside my place still needing to be loaded, readying myself to be rude to someone.

I pull open the door and freeze when my eyes land on him. "Asher?" I whisper and blink a few times, wondering if I'm seeing things.

He gives me a smile that under any other circumstances would set my heart a flutter. But today…a day when I told him I could do this alone, he's apparently decided otherwise. "Hey, beautiful."

The surprise on my face morphs into annoyance. I narrow my eyes and cross my arms over my chest. "What are you doing here?" My words come out sharp and unwelcoming, exactly how I want them to sound.

He lifts his backpack a little higher on his shoulder, keeping his hand around the strap. "Figured you could use a road-trip buddy."

I lean to the side until my shoulder comes to a rest against the doorframe. "You can't be serious," I mutter, but obviously, he is since he's here.

I'm in total disbelief and shock. I've never had a man disregard my words as quickly and easily as Asher Gallo seems to have done.

"I said I would be fine."

He nods. "I know. You're a grown-ass woman."

"I am." I grind my teeth together, trying to control the little bit of sanity I'm somehow maintaining. "I can do a short road trip alone. Hell, I've driven across the entire country with no one except myself."

"But why would you want to, when you have me?" His face is sincere when he utters that statement. "I mean, we could make it fun as hell. Ever been to New Orleans?"

I want to be mad. I really do. I want to put a stop to his macho bullshit as soon as possible, but he's entirely too sweet, and the thought of hitting New Orleans with him sounds like it might actually be a good time.

"No," I whisper, hating myself for wanting to give in and let go of any anger I have toward him in this moment. "I've never been, but I wasn't planning on stopping there on my trip."

"You game for a night of decadence and sin?"

I stare at him, soaking in his good looks and devilish smile. I want to stay mad at him, but he makes it so damn hard. "I'm game."

"Good," he says and starts to take a step toward me.

I hold out my arm, putting up my hand. "But let's get one thing straight."

He nods, not saying a word.

"You pull a stunt like this again, and we're going to be over before we even get going."

"Fair enough," he says without his smile faltering for even the briefest of moments. "It won't happen again."

"It better not," I mumble as I drop my arm back down and move to the side to let him into my place.

His eyes scan my living room as I close the door, cursing at myself under my breath.

"Everything's gone."

"Yep. Just have some stuff in my car and the rest is on its way to a storage warehouse in Tampa until I'm ready for it."

"I thought you'd need my muscle."

I roll my eyes and shake my head. "You had a lot of wrong thoughts."

He turns toward me and drops his backpack near his feet. "I'm sorry," he says softly. "I thought I was doing something good. I thought I was being romantic and sweet, but based on all the things my sister and cousins said this morning, I'm a total asshole."

I've known a lot of assholes in my life, and Asher isn't one of them. He didn't listen to me when I said I could do the trip alone, but he's not an asshole for that. A little overbearing, but not an uncaring jerk. An asshole wouldn't even give a shit about my driving alone or my safety.

"You're not an asshole, Asher. Am I pissed?" I wobble my head like I'm debating. "A little, but there're worse things than a friend showing up to help me drive a thousand miles."

He stalks toward me and wraps an arm around my waist before cupping my face in his palm. "A friend?"

I stare up into his brown eyes, mesmerized by the depth. I swallow, the closeness of him making all the memories of our night together come rushing back.

He brushes his thumb against my cheek, sending goose bumps scattering across my skin. "I'm just a friend?"

I don't say anything. I can't. My body is on

overdrive from the intensity of his gaze and the heat of his body pressed against mine.

"Do most of your friends give you as many orgasms as I do, Olive?" He bends his neck, touching his mouth to mine.

I lean into his kiss, wanting him more than I did the first time we were together.

He pulls away, and I sway forward, trying not to break the connection. "Does a friend kiss you like that? Make you want it like that?"

"No," I whisper, unable to speak any louder.

"You want me?" he taunts me, his face so close I can feel the warmth of his breath against my skin.

"Yes," I breathe as my already racing heart beats faster.

He leans forward, and I close my eyes, waiting and wanting him to touch me…to fuck me.

"In seven hours," he says softly, and my eyes snap open.

"What?"

"You'll have to wait until we get to New Orleans. Good things come to those who wait."

A little growl escapes the back of my throat. "We have time."

He shakes his head as he steps away and takes the warmth of his palm from my face. "We'll have more time once we're there."

"But…"

He shakes his head again. "You ready to get on the road?"

I raise my chin, steeling my spine. "I take it back."

His smile returns, and his eyes light up. "Take what back?"

"You are an asshole."

He laughs with a slow nod. "This asshole is going to make you moan my name later today and beg for more, Olive. Don't ever doubt that. It'll help us make good time and get to our destination a little faster."

"Grr," I snarl, wanting to launch myself at him and do him right on the hardwood floor, but I don't want to give him the satisfaction and anything more to gloat about. "I'm ready to roll."

"Thought so," he says smugly. "This it?" He points toward the small stack of boxes I haven't shoved into my car yet.

"Yep," I snap, annoyed with myself and him.

"I've got this. Do a final check of the place to make sure you didn't forget anything, and I'll meet you outside."

I don't even argue. I want to, though. I want to tell him I can do it myself and that he can wait outside for me. He's managing me again, but I'm so over the move, I don't even care at this point. I have an orgasm waiting in New Orleans, and I can put up with a certain amount of his bullshit to get it.

Asher grabs a few boxes and heads outside. I

stand in the middle of my empty living room still in disbelief.

This is it.

I'm leaving.

Another chapter of my life is over.

Something new is on the horizon, and although I'm excited, I'm scared too.

Change has never been easy for me, but my life has been filled with change at every turn since the first time our parents moved us away from our childhood home.

Now I am returning, putting my roots back down in a place I called home for years.

Good things happened in Texas and in this house. I accomplished so much and worked harder than most people my age. But I am about to step into a new life, a new school, a new dream.

"Hotel booked," Asher says as we ease into the city limits of New Orleans, stuck in a traffic jam that would rival any in Texas.

"Two rooms?"

Asher's hand lands on my leg, right above my knee. "Baby, seriously? One. One room. Can't give you multiple orgasms while in a different room."

"We do have to sleep at some point."

"We'll sleep when we hit Tampa the day after tomorrow."

I turn my head and narrow my eyes. "You mean tomorrow?"

"No. The day after tomorrow. We need to spend at least an entire day in New Orleans, and tonight is fully booked. We're not leaving the room."

"But…"

"Let go, Olive. Life doesn't need to be planned to the very second. Do you have something to do in Tampa tomorrow?"

Damn it. I don't. I was going to Tampa early to spend time with Asher. And I did have my trip planned out just like I do most things in my life until he showed up and tore that to shreds.

"No." I curl my fingers a little tighter around the steering wheel. "I don't have anything."

"Good." He gives my leg a squeeze, making my body come alive with the knowledge that we're almost to our destination and the promised orgasms. "I guarantee we'll have fun."

I think most of Asher's life revolves around fun—something I haven't had much of the last ten years.

"Next exit," he tells me as I'm lost in thought about Asher and fun, two words that are synonymous with each other.

The cars crawl down I-10 until we make it to our exit, and I veer to the right to get out of the mess. I'm thankful we're not driving any farther.

Asher guides me through the city until we pull up in front of a beautiful hotel that looks more like an old French château than a modern hotel.

"It's stunning," I whisper, leaning over the steering wheel to get a better look out the windshield.

"Wait until you see the inside," he tells me, opening the car door. "Nothing but the best for you."

I grab my purse and look up, watching Asher as he runs around the front of the car. "My lady," he says as he opens my door, beating the valet to it. "Your pleasure awaits."

I do my best not to laugh at the ridiculousness, because the last thing I'm doing is blowing up the evening. I want whatever pleasure he's going to give me and even more.

He holds out his hand, and I take it, feeling the familiar zap I get every time we touch. "Thank you."

"For helping you out of the car?" he asks, shutting the car door as soon as I'm a few steps away, handing the keys to the valet.

"For what's about to happen," I say to him, being bolder than I usually am. "I'm hoping I'm unable to talk much later, so I figured I'd cover my bases now."

Asher slides his arm around me, placing his palm on my lower back as he guides me toward the hotel lobby. He leans over, bringing his lips right next to my ear. "If you can talk later, I'm not doing something right."

CHAPTER 13
OLIVE

ASHER'S ARM is around me as we sit on a bench in Jackson Square. He traces circles with his fingertips on the back of my shoulder as we sit in relative silence and people watch. "What do you think?" he asks me.

"Of what?"

"New Orleans."

"It's different, but charming."

He spent hours showing me various places, being a tour guide in a city I'd never been to. But the entire time, I haven't been able to concentrate on much of what he's said because I've been too busy thinking about everything that's happened since he showed up on my doorstep.

"Do you want to stay another day?"

I shake my head as I turn to face him. "I think I want to head to Tampa tomorrow. I'm excited to see my new place and get settled. Is that okay?"

He gives me an easy smile. "It's your trip. Whatever you want."

"I'm supposed to meet the leasing agent to pick up my keys day after tomorrow. And with how long the drive is, I want to at least be in the city so I don't miss my appointment with her."

"And where are you staying tomorrow night?"

"A hotel near campus."

"Cancel it," he tells me.

I jerk my head back and knit my eyebrows together. "I can't cancel it."

"Why not?"

"It's nonrefundable."

"It's probably a shithole if it's near campus."

"It's not. I did my research."

Asher laughs. "The only places near campus are next to strip clubs and don't always charge by the night."

"How do they charge, then?"

He raises an eyebrow. "How do you think?"

"No," I say to him, knowing I researched the place and read the reviews before I booked. "It's not one of those places."

"We'll see," he says smugly, and I can't wait to prove him wrong. "I know my city and that area. Nothing good happens there."

I shrug. "As long as there's a bed to sleep in, I don't care what people do there."

The silence returns as I stare at the church doors

and the few people sitting on the front steps sipping their coffees.

"Why aren't you married yet?" I ask Asher, wondering why he's still single at his age.

"Why aren't you?"

"I've been too busy with school to even date very much, and I didn't want to get attached to someone and become trapped somewhere I didn't want to stay."

"What do you mean?"

I turn my entire body around on the bench as he pulls his arm back. "If I would've fallen for a man from Texas, I would've felt the need to stay there for him. I knew where I wanted to go for my doctorate and what I wanted to focus on. I didn't want to give anyone the chance to steal my dreams."

He studies my face, his eyes roaming around my features. "He would've gone with you."

I roll my eyes at his cluelessness. "Not every man is willing to drop anything for a woman."

"A man who truly loves a woman will move heaven and earth to make sure her dreams come true."

His words are so sweet, but it's hard for me to believe they're based in reality. Asher talks a good game, but I'm not sure he'd follow through. "You'd leave your entire family behind for your girlfriend?"

He winces. "I'd leave my hometown to be with my wife if it meant she was fulfilling her dream."

"But not a girlfriend?"

He sucks in a breath through the corner of his mouth. "It would depend."

"On what?"

"On if she was the one or not."

"And you think you would know that? If she's the one or not?"

His face changes as his eyes light up, and his smile returns. "I do," he says in the smoothest, velvety tone.

I don't know why, but the way he stares at me and says those words has my heart fluttering and my belly doing wicked somersaults.

"You should never settle for anything less than that, Olive." He reaches out his arm and takes my hand in his. "Don't ever settle for mediocrity."

His words make me think. I haven't dated much, but have I always settled when it came to relationships? I definitely haven't had the ability to pick the right men, based on Asher's statement. But I also never felt like I had much to give to the relationships to let them thrive and grow. I was too busy with school and trying to achieve all of my goals. None of that included a boyfriend who could derail my plans and blow up my future.

"Is that why you aren't in a serious relationship?" I ask.

"I am in one," he says, his eyes boring into me with the most serious look on his face.

My mouth instantly goes dry. I swallow, trying to

get rid of the sandpaper coating my throat and tongue. Is he… "Wait," I say, my eyes widening as I realize what he's saying, but it can't be true. "You're seeing someone?"

He can't be talking about me. Sure, we've talked since I left Tampa, but we've barely spent any time together. He said he wants to be in a relationship with me, and I want that too, but maybe I've been played somehow along the way. Weirder shit has happened.

He tightens his hand around mine. "I'm looking at her."

"Asher," I whisper.

"I was waiting for the right girl. Someone who I thought was worthy of my love and time. Someone who wanted nothing from me except my company. That's you, Olive. Hell, you didn't even want my help moving halfway across the country."

"But here you are," I say with a half smile, still stunned by his previous statement.

"I watched you walk away once without following through on how I felt. I'm not about to do that again. I'm taking no chances when it comes to us and what could be—should be our future."

"I don't share, Asher."

"I wouldn't ask you to. I don't share either, Olive."

We stare at each other as the world moves around us. Tourists stroll by as the weight of the words we've just spoken seep in deep.

"Can you be a one-woman man?"

He nods. "It's in my DNA."

I snort and stop myself from rolling my eyes at him again. "It's literally not."

He shrugs a shoulder. "I can be a one-woman man. No one has ever made me want to, though, until you came back into my life. Now—" he clears his throat, moving closer to me on the bench "—can we move on to better topics?"

I nod. "Like what?"

"Let's talk about orgasms."

This time, I don't hold back and roll my eyes. "What about them?"

"How many have you had since we got to New Orleans?"

"I don't know…three."

He jerks his body back like I hit him. "You don't know?"

"No. No. I do know. It's three."

I wasn't keeping count, and each one happened quicker and easier than the previous one. I'd always been so stressed about having an orgasm that I'd often make it impossible for my body to relax enough to push myself over the edge. But there's something about the way Asher looks at me and touches me that puts my mind at ease.

"We're going to at least double that number before we get on the road in the morning."

My breath rushes out of my body. "I don't think my body can handle that much."

"Oh, it can," he says with a wink and a sinful smile.

If I were standing, my knees would be weak, and my legs would give out from under me. The man has the ability to suck all the strength out of me with a simple phrase or a single look.

"I don't—"

He lifts his hand and places a finger against my lips. "Trust me," he says softly.

I nod, trusting him more than any other man I've dated. But what would I have to lose? He's talking about giving me orgasms and more pleasure than anyone else has ever tried to give me before.

He stands and holds out his hand to me. I slide my palm into his, my legs a little weak as he pulls me to my feet. I fall forward, our chests colliding, but Asher catches me with an arm around my back. I tip my head back, staring up into his haunting dark eyes as we stand outside St. Louis Cathedral.

"Do you believe in fate or destiny?" he asks me, holding me tightly against him.

"I don't know," I tell him honestly. The scientist part of my brain says it's an impossibility, but the way my heart beats when I'm around Asher proves otherwise.

"I believe in it," he whispers, and my breath catches.

I've loved Asher Gallo since the first time I laid eyes on him. Sure, I was a kid, but I was drawn to him, and that didn't go away until well after we moved.

He bends his neck and pulls me closer as his lips land on mine, stealing what little air is left in my lungs. The world around us ceases to exist. Everything goes quiet as I give in to his kiss, opening my lips, and sliding my tongue against his. The way his mouth presses against mine is both demanding and sweet, a perfect mix that makes my heart beat faster and has my body craving more.

When he pulls away, breaking our kiss, the world around us slowly comes back into focus like I'm being pulled out of a dream.

"Care to have your fortune told?" an old woman sitting at a fold-up card table nearby asks us. "I can answer all your questions."

"What?" I ask, my mind still a hazy blur.

The woman smiles as she sits before a half-burned candle. She looks exactly how you'd picture an old fortune-teller. Her hair is wrapped in a colorful scarf, with long gray strands spilling out and cascading down her shoulders. She has on large costume jewelry that's hard to miss even in the dim light of the French Quarter at night.

"Care to know your future?" The woman motions toward the empty seat across from her. "I can tell you everything."

"I don't believe in telling the future," I say, still wrapped in Asher's arms.

"Are you scared?" he teases me.

"I'm scared of nothing." I'm lying, of course. The only thing in this world that scares me is Asher and what the future holds for us. No matter how much I want to believe there's more of our story to be written, I wonder if it'll be filled with love or tragedy.

I pull out of Asher's arms and move toward the empty seat.

The old woman stares at Asher, paying me no attention. "We need privacy," she tells him. "Give us ten minutes."

Asher's gaze moves to me, and I nod. "I'll be okay."

I've never had my fortune read or even had the smallest inkling to sit down and hear what a mystic had to say. But there's something about being in New Orleans, surrounded by all the tales of this being the supernatural epicenter.

"Ten minutes," he says before walking away slowly.

"Your hand, my dear," the woman says, placing her arm on the table with her palm facing up. "I'll read your lines."

I give her my hand and settle in to be told nothing more than an interesting fairy tale. I'm sure if I sat in this area all night, I'd hear the same story repeated time after time to every paying customer.

"Interesting," the old woman mutters, running her fingertip across my palm. "This is your love line."

It's not hard for her to start off with my love life. She watched Asher and me kiss. Naturally, I'm taken and maybe even a little bit in love.

I stay quiet, not wanting to give her any information.

"You've had your heart broken before."

This isn't a big stretch. Every person my age has had at least one heartache and failed relationship. I don't know anyone who makes it out of their teens or early twenties without a small scar on their heart.

"But it's a different type of broken heart," she explains, moving her face closer to my hand like she's trying to read the small notes I find at the bottom of a page in my textbooks. "There was a break in time but not feelings. Something kept you two apart. Something out of your control, but you've somehow found your way back to each other."

My mind starts to spin. I think back to what we were talking about on the bench and wonder if she overheard our conversation. There's no way she'd know this type of information unless she was eavesdropping.

"And?" I ask, unable to stop myself from wanting to know more. Do I believe? No, but that doesn't mean I don't want to hear the rest of the tale she is about to weave.

My gaze wanders to Asher as he strolls around the square and looks at the art that's hanging on the black wrought-iron fence. He looks so relaxed and unbothered by everything and everyone around him. Every time I'm with him, he's like that, and it's the same way he was in high school. It's as if he glides through life, and the people and things orbit around him, instead of the other way around.

"Your line is solid after this point." She taps my palm in an area where the line is, in fact, intact from that point forward. "You will be lucky in love going forward in your life."

"So, he's the one?" I ask her, playing along with the charade.

She nods. "He is, indeed. He's always been the one, but you had a few other avenues to take before you were brought back into his path."

"Anything else?" I ask her.

"Your lifeline is long. You'll live to an old age, surrounded by—" she turns my hand to the side, studying another set of lines "—many, many children."

"Many, many? How many is many, many?" For a moment, I feel a sense of panic, and my palms begin to sweat more than they were from the damp night air in the South. But then I remember, this is all nonsense. Her information isn't real. It's just a way for her to score money from tourists.

"I can't be sure, but more than three."

She can't be sure.

That's the truest thing she's said to me since I sat down. Well, besides Asher being out of my life and having come back in. Those were all guesses or part of an overheard conversation she had no business listening to.

"Thank you," I tell her and pull my hand out of her grip to grab the money she wants. That was the point of all this. It's a bit of entertainment on my part, but it's her way of life and the means to feed herself.

When I slide the twenty across the table, she places her hand on top of mine, trapping it. "One more thing, deary."

I resist the urge to yank my hand away. "What?" I ask.

"Your life isn't going to go as planned. There will be obstacles and big changes coming soon, but you'll get over them when you realize you aren't in control of your destiny."

"Okay," I mutter as she releases my hand and stuffs the twenty-dollar bill into her bra. "Duly noted."

"Do you think your man would like a reading?" she asks.

"No. He's good. We're in a hurry."

The woman smiles and nods, plucking a small feather from a bag on the side of her table. "Take this as a remembrance of what was said today. You may not find the information useful now, but soon, you'll understand."

I reluctantly take the feather from her, shoving the

shaft into the small pocket on the side of my purse. “Thank you.”

“Have a wonderful evening,” she says to me with a slight bow of her head.

Asher’s eyes meet mine as I stand. I’m momentarily breathless, dumb struck at how quickly my life has changed. New city. New school. Newish man. My life is already being turned on end. So, that statement she made has already come true.

“You ready?” Asher says as he walks up to me.

“Yeah.” I clutch his arm. “More than ready.”

“What did she say?”

“A bunch of nonsense,” I explain, but I’m not sure what else to say. She wasn’t really wrong about anything, but it was general enough that it could fit most people’s lives.

“I need more specifics.”

I shake my head. “It’s not important.”

“I’ll get it out of you eventually.”

I peer up at him as we walk through the square. “You will?”

“I have my ways, and all of them are fun.”

I giggle at his ridiculousness. “You’re weird.”

“Have you ever been tied up?” he asks with a raised eyebrow.

“Um, what?”

He smirks, and I know I don’t want to know, but I have a feeling I’m going to find out.

CHAPTER 14
ASHER

"WHAT IN THE ACTUAL FUCK?" Olive whispers, holding her backpack in her hand as she stands in the doorway to her hotel room.

I peer over her shoulder, getting a good look at the room. Sheesh. It's a mess, and the cockroaches crawling all over the walls and the carpet are the icing on the cake. I don't want to say I told her so, but I told her so. The motels and hotels in this area are notorious for being shitholes.

"I've never seen anything like it," I tease her. "I mean, it's not too bad if you don't mind things crawling on you all night."

The glare she gives me is deadly. "I don't think I've ever seen a place like this."

"Why would you want to?"

She chews on the corner of her mouth, letting her

eyes do another pass as the baby cockroaches climb up the wall, making an interesting design.

"I'm so pissed. Now I have to find another hotel for the night."

I smirk. "Or you can…"

She turns around, the bugs a weird backdrop as they keep moving. "I can what?"

"Stay with me for the night."

She exhales. "Okay."

"Okay?" I raise my eyebrows, figuring she'd put up more of a fight and make me work for it a little bit more.

"Yeah. I can't stay here." She waves her hand toward the room. "As long as you don't have bugs, then I'm game."

"No bugs," I promise her, taking her backpack from her hands. "Let's get out of here."

She doesn't even bother closing the door before she starts to walk toward the side exit where her car is parked. "I'm too tired to fight with anyone. I need a hot bath and a long sleep."

I rush in front of her, pushing open the door. "I have a comfortable bed and a big tub."

As soon as she steps outside, she turns to face me and continues walking backward. "You're talking dirty to me, Asher." She has a smirk on her face as she speaks. "You're truly outdoing yourself."

"Your wish is my command," I say teasingly, but if I had my way, she'd stay more than the night.

In all my years, I've never spent so much time with another woman that I'm not related to. I've never allowed it. Time means feelings, and I haven't been interested in planting any seeds that could or would grow into anything more.

But maybe I was waiting…waiting for Olive. Why didn't I track her down sooner? Why didn't she reach out to me? We were friends in school, and before she left, she promised she'd always stay in contact.

I toss her stuff in the back with mine as my mind fills with so many questions that I'll never have the answer to. "I'll drive," I tell her and rush toward the driver's side of the car before she has a chance to get in. "It'll be easier since I know where I'm going."

She stares at me, holding the keys in her hand. "I haven't forgotten how to get to places around here. I spent more of my life in this area than out of it."

She may not have forgotten the place, but for a while at least, she forgot the people—more specifically, me. "Why don't you sit back and relax and let me do the last leg of this trip?"

Her gaze doesn't move from mine as she reaches out, placing the keys in my hand. "Fine," she breathes before it turns into a yawn, and she quickly covers her mouth. "I'm almost too tired to think."

"I got you, baby," I tell her, ticking my chin toward the other side of the car. "Get in. Let's go. There's a bathtub and a bed with your name on it."

We're halfway to my place when I can no longer

hold in some of the questions I've had on my mind. "Why didn't you ever call or write?"

She turns her head toward me, her eyes half hooded from exhaustion. "I don't know. I figured you didn't want to hear from me."

"Olive." I shake my head, returning my eyes to the road. "You promised me you'd call."

"So did you."

Damn.

She has a point. We both made that promise, and we both dropped the ball. It wasn't a one-way street, but I had somehow started to paint it that way in my mind.

"I assumed it was just something you said when someone moved away. I didn't think you actually meant it. I waited to see if you'd reach out first, and when you didn't, I figured I was right. They were hollow words and promises."

"I thought the same."

She presses the back of her head into the seat and slowly nods. "And then time happened. I looked you up a few times on social media."

I glance her way, surprised by her admission. "You did?"

"Yeah. I typed out a few messages, but I'd chicken out and never send them."

If I am honest, I looked her up too. At least in the beginning when I wanted to know what was going on with her. But then I stopped going on certain apps, and time moved on, putting Olive in the back of my mind instead of at the front.

"I made new friends and figured this part of my life—" she waves her hand toward the window "—was over and that I needed to move on. I was so sad for so long that I made myself not dwell on what I left behind. It was too painful and stopped me from moving forward."

"You were that sad?" I ask her, not understanding what it would be like to go through what she did.

"You know I don't have a family like yours. My entire world was my friends…our friend group. And when I moved away, I felt like I lost everything. Everyone says they're going to stay in contact and that you'll be friends forever, but it's all empty promises. No one ever stays as connected as you are when you see each other every day. I was alone. I had to make new friends, which isn't as easy in high school. I had River, but he's about as much fun as a porcupine under attack."

I snort, never having liked her brother. Maybe because he hated my being friends with his sister. He always thought I was trying to get in her pants, and he wasn't entirely wrong, but it never happened. Until now.

"I finally feel like I'm home again. No place has ever felt right since I left here. This area will always have my heart."

"Will you stay after school?" I ask, needing to

know in order to figure out where we could go in this relationship.

If I have my way, she'll stay, and we'll ride this out for as long as she can possibly stand me.

She nods. "I can't imagine living anywhere else. If I have my way, I'll be here forever."

A sense of relief washes over me. I haven't allowed myself to think about what she is going to do after grad school. I have been more excited about having her now, and I haven't thought about much beyond that point. "Good."

"Do you want me to stay?" she whispers. "After grad school?"

"I do," I tell her honestly.

"Good. I wasn't going anywhere. I refuse to lose the sunsets."

"Only the sunsets?" I ask, peering over at her while stopped at a red light.

She smirks. "No."

"Good girl."

Her smirk changes into a smile as her cheeks turn pink. "Don't," she mumbles.

"Don't what?"

"Don't say that."

"Why?"

She ticks her head toward the street. "The light is green."

I ease off the brake and press the gas pedal. "Why?" I ask again.

"It's weird."

"Based on the way the color in your face changed, I'd say you liked it."

"Stop," she pleads, turning her face toward the passenger window and hiding it from view.

I had her. She likes praise. I'll remember that later and use it to my advantage.

"We're only a few minutes away." I ignore my phone as it goes off, my family being annoying and nosy.

"Good. Your phone is going crazy."

My phone buzzes again. "Ignore it."

"Aren't you worried something is wrong?"

I shake my head. "It's my cousins being assholes."

"I know and remember all of them, and they're not assholes. They're sweet."

"You'll learn soon enough that they've changed."

Olive laughs. "You're lucky to have them."

"I'll remember you said that when they're being nosy and rude."

As I turn onto my street, I instantly see the one thing I hadn't planned.

"Wow. Someone must be having a party," Olive says, taking in the cars lining the street.

"Nope," I snap, tightening my grip on the steering wheel. "It's the assholes."

"What? Oh my gosh. Why?"

"You. Me. And being nosy assholes."

She laughs again. "Stop calling them that."

"Why do you think they're here? I didn't invite them."

"To see you, of course. You're being silly."

I pull into the driveway, and half of the cousins are outside. I assume the other half are inside my house. Fucking Tamara. She has a key, and I can guarantee she made herself at home.

"They thought you'd kick my ass when I showed up at your door."

"I thought about it." Olive reaches for the door handle, but I grab her arm, stopping her.

"I'm glad you didn't."

"Me too. Your face is kind of nice."

"Kind of?" I ask, pulling her over to kiss her lips. "You're spicy tonight."

She smiles against my lips. "Have my back in there, okay?"

"I'll have your back everywhere and always, Oli."

She takes a deep breath as she pulls away from me. "I can do this. They're nice and not assholes," she tells herself.

"I thought you knew everyone?" I tease her, using her words against her.

She reaches across the console and smacks my arm. "Don't be a jerk."

The front door opens, and Tamara steps outside, placing her hand above her eyes to get a better view inside the car with the sunlight shining on her face.

"Ready?" I ask Olive.

She nods and reaches for the door handle, exiting the car before I have a chance to climb out the driver's side.

"Hey," she says to Tamara, striding up the driveway like she wasn't giving herself a pep talk only a few seconds ago.

"Well, aren't you a sight for sore eyes," Tamara says and grabs Olive, pulling her into a giant hug. "How did the road trip go?"

"Great. Great," Olive says. "Better than expected."

"What are you all doing here?" I ask, walking up behind Olive. "How did you know we were on our way here?"

Tamara steps away from my girl and crosses her arms as she leans against the side of the porch. "Your location service is turned on. We were tracking you and wanted to be here to hear all about your trip. We missed you."

"That's so sweet," Olive says as she slides her arm around my back and smashes herself into my side.

I peer down at her before I close my eyes and take a deep breath. When I open them again, I look up at my sister as she stands on my front porch. "You all missed me? And how the hell did you track me?"

Stone raises his hand. "You shared your location with me a while back. Guess it never stopped."

"Fucking hell," I mutter under my breath. "And you decided to share it with everyone?"

"Don't be a pussy," Stone tells me as Opal sits on his lap, looking happier than ever. "You know there're no secrets."

"I'm surprised you all didn't have a drone following me."

Tamara tilts her head. "Damn. I didn't even think of that, but it's a good idea."

"Stop it," I tell her, shooting her a glare. "I hope you at least brought some food. We haven't had dinner yet."

"Yep. I went down to Bread and Butter and got all your favorites."

My stomach instantly growls. "You're forgiven," I tell her as we walk up the steps and join half the family on the porch.

"Well, come on, then," Tamara says, motioning for us to follow her into my own house.

"Your place is so cute," Olive says at my side as we step inside.

"I wasn't going for cute, but thanks," I tell her.

Olive slides her arm out from behind me and kicks off her shoes in the entryway. "Did you decorate it yourself?"

"No." My eyes meet those of my sister, who has a shit-eating grin on her face.

"I helped or else it would be a mishmash of old college furniture and white walls." Tamara walks up to Olive and takes her arm, pulling her deeper into the house.

"You okay, bro?" Mammoth asks, smacking me on the back. "You're still in one piece."

"She didn't kick my ass, but it was pretty damn hairy there for a hot second."

He laughs and shakes his head. "Olive's a patient woman. You better lock her down."

"Done."

Mammoth's eyebrows rise. "Yeah?"

"Yeah. We're going to ride this out and see what happens."

"Ride it out and lock it down. Don't wait for shit to go haywire and let fate take her away. You got me?"

I nod and gaze across the living room to Olive and Tamara. "I got you, brother. Loud and clear."

He places a hand on my shoulder, stepping into my sightline. "You start fucking it up, dropping the ball"—his eyes bore into me—"and I'm going to rein you back in and remind you to get your head out of your ass."

"I won't fuck it up."

He squeezes the muscle near my neck. "Damn right, you won't. I won't allow it."

I glare at him, loving and hating him at the same time. "Calm your shit. I got this, old man."

Mammoth tips his head back and laughs before he rights himself and playfully slaps my cheek. "Asshole."

CHAPTER 15
OLIVE

"I LOVE YOUR FAMILY." I lean my head against Asher's shoulder as we sit around the table on his back patio, overlooking the Gulf, surrounded by his cousins.

"They're okay," he replies, but I know he doesn't mean it. He loves each one of them, and no matter what he says, he can't hide that fact from me.

"As much as we love and missed you, we're here about another issue," his cousin Gigi announces as she rises from the table. "And it requires a group approach."

"What's the issue that requires an unofficial family meeting?" Asher asks.

I'm suddenly curious to watch the inner workings of his family. Mine discusses nothing as a group, even though there are only the four of us.

"It's Tate," Tamara says.

"She's kind of far away to be a problem," Asher says. "And the last time I checked, she's a fully grown woman."

Tamara crosses her arms over her chest and narrows her eyes at her brother. "That doesn't mean she doesn't need our help. In fact, she reached out to Gigi and asked for it."

Asher's body jerks back ever so slightly. Not enough for other people to see, but I feel the movement. "She called and asked for help?"

Tamara nods with a closed-lipped sarcastic smile. "Yep," she snaps.

"Fuck," Asher mutters.

"Yeah," Lily says.

"What the hell happened?" Nick asks. "You didn't give us the whole story yet, Tam."

"I wanted to wait until we were all together before we discussed her issue."

"Well, here we are," Asher says to his sister. "And it's getting late."

"It's nine o'clock," Rebel teases. "Someone's getting old."

"And we've been on the road for ten hours. I'm not old, Reb. I'm tired."

Rebel shrugs. "Whatever you say, honey."

"Tate," Rosie says, bringing the conversation back to where it needs to be.

Gigi starts to pace before she speaks. "Tate's been

in a relationship with a badass motorcycle dude in Chicago."

"Been there, done that," Tamara mumbles.

"He got popped by the Feds on some RICO charges. The guys from his club think she had something to do with it, and her man can't do shit about that from behind bars. She's running until things get cleared up."

"Damn," Luna whispers.

"Fucking hell," Asher says. "Where's she headed?"

"Here," Gigi replies. "This is the safest place for her. Uncle James and Uncle Thomas will take some time to figure shit out for her, and in the meantime, she'll need to hop from house to house so she isn't in one place too long. The more she moves, the harder it will be for them to find her and will buy us time."

"Damn," Pike, Gigi's husband, whispers. "This shit is bad."

"It's fucked up," Mammoth mutters and reaches for Tamara's hand, giving it a squeeze. "But we'll keep her safe."

Asher leans over, placing his mouth near my ear. "Pike and Mammoth were both wrapped up with clubs back in the day."

My eyes widen as my gaze turns toward them. "No way."

"Way," he says.

"Is it that asshole who was at your wedding, Rocco?" Trace asks.

Rocco nods. "Same asshat."

"What the hell was his name? Ruckus?" Trace tilts his head up, moving his gaze around the sky like the answer was up there somehow. "Or maybe it was Riot."

"Rowdy," Luna spits out. "His name was Rowdy."

"That's it," Rocco says, scrunching up his face. "The fucker looked like trouble even then."

"They've been together for a long time," Rebel says. "She has to be a mess."

"We're about to find out," Tamara says. "She'll be here tomorrow."

My head is spinning with all this information. It's like a television drama filled with danger, romance, and intrigue.

"We'll handle it," Lily says as she pushes off the sofa. She walks to the window that faces the front yard. "Jett and I will take her the first few nights."

"We'll take her second," Gigi adds.

"Should we write down a schedule?" Tamara asks.

I watch in amazement as they discuss a plan and work out a schedule that will work for everyone when it comes to Tate. I can't imagine growing up with a support system like this. It absolutely blows my mind. I've had River and no one else, but I feel like if I had the Gallos, I could conquer the world.

"Are you okay?" Asher asks, squeezing my hand.

I turn my gaze away from his family to look at him. "I am. I'm good."

"Where did you go to in your head?"

I smile at him. "I've never been around everyone in one place, working through a problem. It's fascinating to watch your family at work."

"It's usually a hot mess."

"A hot mess is better than having no one."

Asher leans over, hooking his arms underneath me before I have a chance to react. I squeak as he lifts me inches off the couch and onto his lap, settling me against him like I weigh nothing.

I freeze when his hot breath caresses my ear. "You'll never be alone again, Olive. You have me and them."

I peer up, surveying the group, wondering if I could ever be fully accepted into the family. The spouses seem to have slid right in, and if I hadn't known the family before, I wouldn't have been able to pick out who was blood or not based on how they acted.

"I love that," I whisper.

"I hope you're okay with this," Rosie says, and when I don't respond, she elbows me gently. "Olive, are you okay with this?"

"With what?" I ask, momentarily distracted by Asher's chuckling against my ear.

"With Tate possibly staying here."

My eyebrows rise high and fast. "It's Asher's place."

Rosie's eyebrows do the exact opposite, drawing together tightly. "But you're staying here."

"Only for the night." I give her a smile and add in a shrug because it's weird that she's asking if I'm okay with Tate being around.

"Oh." Her eyebrows rise as her eyes widen. "Why?"

"Why what?" I ask, confused.

She leans over, speaking in a softer tone as the rest of the family continues on with their conversation about how to keep Tate's ass alive and untouched. "Why are you only staying the night?"

"I have a place I rented closer to campus."

"Why?" she asks again with a serious face and her eyebrows still knitted. "Asher's place is beautiful."

"We're new."

"So?"

"It's his place."

"It's big, though."

My body shakes as Asher laughs underneath me. "It is," I tell her and shift on his lap until my bottom presses against his cock, shutting him up quickly. "But we're not at that point yet in our relationship."

"Thank fuck," Asher mutters, "She finally admits it's a relationship."

I peer over my shoulder at him and smirk.

Rosie's warm hand lands on my forearm, drawing

my attention away from Asher. "But why pay rent when you can live here with your man?"

"Rosie, we're not there yet," I explain again, hoping to kill this line of questioning.

"And when will you know when you are there?" she asks, her head tilted as she stares at me with an unsettling look.

When will I know? Is there ever a time a person knows everything is right? For as smart as I am, I don't have a clue.

"We'll see how things go. I already signed a yearlong lease. If Asher hasn't grown bored of me by then, we'll cross that bridge when the time comes."

Rosie snickers. "Sweetheart, you don't quite understand how the men in this family love, do you?"

"Men in this family love differently?"

My question has Asher tightening his hold across my stomach, pulling me closer to his body.

"Damn right, they do. If you got this far, you're in. A man, especially a Gallo, doesn't fly halfway across the country, only to then sit in a car for the same number of miles for someone they don't plan to go the distance with."

"They do for their friends," I tell her.

"You two have sex?" she throws back.

My smile tightens, but I don't answer.

"You screw all your friends?" she asks with one eyebrow raised and her arms folded.

"No."

"No to having sex with Asher, or no to screwing your friends?"

Damn.

I've heard the term nosy Rosie, and they had to have come up with it after having a conversation with Rosie Gallo.

"That's enough, Ro," Asher says softly but with an edge. "Leave the woman be. She's had a long day. And if she wants to pay for an apartment she'll never be at, that's on her and none of your business."

"I'll be there." I look at him over my shoulder again. "I need to sleep somewhere."

Asher gives me a smug smirk. "Baby, you're going to be sleeping in my bed, or I'm going to be sleeping in yours."

This man must be delusional. While he's the bonus to moving here, I picked this area for the university and to finish my education. I refuse to let myself get lost and sidetracked by anything—especially a man—even if it is Asher Gallo.

"Not all the time," I argue. "We don't live that close. You have work, and I have school."

"Oh boy," Rosie whispers. "Here we go."

"We'll talk about it later," Asher says, flattening his hand against my stomach.

He's shutting me down in the nicest way possible, but it's still not acceptable. I want to argue with him and hash it out now, but I don't want to do it in front of his family.

"If you want to finish it now, I'll grab some popcorn," Rosie teases.

"Later," Asher says softly from behind me.

"You were always the one person I could count on for a good time and stirring the drama pot." Rosie gives him a very dramatic pout. "You're turning into such a fun killer, Ash."

"I like stirring up everyone else's drama, Ro, not my own."

I chew my lip, staring across the room, processing everything that Asher's said. Maybe his other women have spent time in his bed without a moment away from each other, but I've never been that type of girl. Even when I dated someone, I wasn't a sleepover type of person. I liked my space and studying was my top priority for years…even more than sleep.

"We better go. You two have had a long day," Gigi says as she gazes down at us. "You coming to the shop tomorrow?"

"I'll be there," Asher tells her.

"Good. Your first appointment isn't until four, so you can get some rest."

"I know, Gi. I looked at my calendar earlier. I'll be there in plenty of time to prep my station."

She smiles at him and then turns her attention to me. "We're happy you're back and that you found Asher again. You two are good together."

I smile, wondering how she'd know. "You think?"

She nods. "I thought you two would hook up before you moved away, but it never happened."

I snort. "I wasn't exactly his type back then."

Gigi shakes her head. "Yes, you were."

"Gigi," Asher warns.

She lifts her hands and backs away. "I'm going. I'll save it all for another day." With her hands still raised, she waves them around and whistles. "Let's go. They need some time to rest."

"Yeah, sure," Tamara says with a chuckle. "I'm sure they're going to rest."

Her husband, Mammoth, slings his arm around her shoulders and moves her toward the front door. "Come on, sweetheart. We need to rest too. Your parents still have the kids for another hour."

"Bye," Lily says as she walks by, following Mammoth and Tamara out the front door with her husband right behind her.

"Later," Jett calls out, waving over his head.

"We'll see you tomorrow," Pike says to Asher with a chin lift and gives me a smile with a head nod.

Quick goodbyes come from everyone else as they walk out the front door until there's an eerie quiet in the house. I didn't realize how loud they all were when they talked until it was just us.

I slide to the side and off Asher's lap. "Are you worried about your cousin?"

Asher shifts until he's facing me. "Tate?"

I nod.

"Nah. My uncles will figure something out."

"Well, that's good." I pull at the hem of my sundress, covering my knees.

When we were on the road trip, being alone with Asher didn't feel awkward. But now, after his remarks about where we'd be sleeping, there's a weird vibe between us.

"Want to talk about it now?" he asks like he's reading my mind. "Or save it for another day?"

I gaze down at my legs and swallow, wondering if it's smart to have our first real fight already and if I'm ready for the ramifications of whatever the outcome is. I peer up at him, meeting his gaze. "If you want to, or we can wait."

He leans back against the armrest of his couch, tucking his ankle underneath one leg. "I'd rather talk about it now so we can move on to something else."

"Okay," I whisper.

"You don't want to spend the nights together? Our days are going to be busy, but our nights will be free. It may be the only real time we get to spend together."

"Some nights."

He cocks his head, studying my face. "How many?"

I think about it and blurt out, "Two."

He shakes his head immediately. "Five."

I jerk my head back in shock. "That's a little much, no?"

His eyes narrow, and he cocks his head the other way. "I want seven. I was trying to be giving."

"Giving?" I bark out a laugh. "Giving is two, Asher."

"Again, I want seven."

"That's every day."

"I know." He smirks. "Why is that so absurd?"

I shrug a shoulder and settle into the seat cushion, letting my back rest against the pillow behind me. "We both have our own lives."

"Baby," he says, reaching out to take my hand. "I spent too many years without you to not be together every moment we can."

"You're going to get sick of me."

No one has ever spent that much time with me. Not even the man I had the longest relationship with. He said I was too dull to be around that much because I liked to study, and he was bored.

"I'm really not that much fun, Asher. I study a lot. Like a lot, a lot. What are you going to do all night while I study?"

"Draw like I always do. I spend hours every night preparing for my upcoming clients who want custom designs."

"You don't go out at night?" I ask, surprised he spends his evenings working.

"I used to when I was younger and had Stone to hang out with. But now…now, I come home, relax, make dinner, and work on my designs."

"Huh."

"Huh, what?"

"I'm just surprised, is all."

"I had to grow up sometime."

The man is full of surprises, and I know there is a lot I still have to learn. "Can we start with two and adjust from there?"

He exhales. "As long as we adjust up. I'm not adjusting down."

"Fine," I say, giving in for now. "What time do you work until?"

"Some nights are late, but I'm usually home by eight. We've been better about closing the shop earlier since everyone has little ones at home."

"Eight?"

He nods. "Yeah. It's sweet."

"What time were you open until?"

"Back in the day, the shop was open until midnight."

"Damn. That is late."

"I'm glad we don't do that grind anymore."

"I'll stay over the nights you're going to be earlier."

"I'm my own boss, Olive. I can make every night an early night whenever I want."

I shake my head. "I really need time alone for school, Ash. No matter how badly I want to be with you, school comes before anything else."

"Even me?" He touches his chest and frowns. "I should feel hurt by that comment."

"I don't think you understand how boring I really am, Asher."

He pulls my arms, causing me to fall forward into him. "I think you think I'm still sixteen and need to be constantly entertained. I'm not that kid anymore, Oli. I like boring. I want boring." He places a finger underneath my chin, forcing my gaze to meet his. "Whatever you got, wherever you are, I want to be there."

"Don't say I didn't warn you," I whisper as he tips his head down, bringing those luscious lips closer to me.

"Shut up and kiss me," he commands.

My breath hitches at his words.

He's so bossy, but there's something about the way he stares at me that makes me want more.

CHAPTER 16
ASHER

"COUSIN," Tate says, leaping into my arms as soon as I walk into Inked.

She looks older than the last time I saw her, finally getting rid of her baby face.

"Hey Tater Tot," I say, wrapping my arms around her. "What's up, troublemaker?"

She laughs as she plops down, her boots making a loud thud against the shop floor. "You know how we do." She gives me the biggest smile and punches me playfully in the shoulder.

"Not me, kid. I'm out of that game."

She pouts. "Not you too."

I shrug and tip my hands upward. "The adulting gig isn't all it's cracked up to be."

"That ain't no lie, cousin." She peers over her shoulder, checking to see who's around. When she realizes we're alone, she whispers, "and this crew is no longer as much fun as I thought they were either. They're old as fuck."

"It happens to the best of us." I reach out my hand and ruffle her hair, something she's always hated but has come to expect from me. "So, tell me what happened? Why's your ass here in Florida, and why in the hell are you wearing that black leather jacket in this heat?"

She twirls as she fixes her hair and drops her ass into the chair at the front desk. "Rowdy's a dumb fuck."

"Tell me something I don't already know." I lean an elbow against the desk, trying to extract as much information as I can out of her. "Want to expound on that?"

She sighs, resting her elbow on the desk, and places her chin in her palm. "He's being framed."

I roll my eyes at that statement. "You're talking to me, Tate. Rowdy has never lived his life on the up-and-up."

The last time I saw her, I'd gone up to Chicago to visit the family and party in the city. I met Rowdy only briefly, but everything about him screamed criminal. I don't know how Angelo let his daughter date such an obvious asshole.

"He's not a bad guy," she tells me, like I'm a moron who's going to buy her story about how her low-life biker boyfriend is really a knight in shining armor.

"How long have you two been together?"

"A long time."

"How old were you when you started dating?"

"When we really started dating, or when I told my parents we started dating?"

I hang my head out of mental exhaustion. She's a trying one. If I had a daughter like her, I'd probably lock her in her room every night in order to keep my sanity. "When you really started dating."

"Sixteen."

I mutter a slew of curse words under my breath.

"He thought I was twenty-one, though."

It takes everything in me not to roll my eyes at the stupidity of what she just said. "Tate, you looked like you were sixteen until last year. You can't feed that bullshit to me."

She pushes her breasts together, smashing the logo from Guns N' Roses, making it unreadable. "I've had these tits forever, and they aren't those of a sixteen-year-old."

"Then they were, in fact, the tits of a sixteen-year-old."

"It's not his fault. I always looked older."

Lies. All lies. There's no way a man, fully grown, dated a sixteen-year-old and was completely clueless about her age. I remember how sixteen-year-olds act, and it is nowhere near as mature as someone who's twenty-one. God, even a twenty-one-year-old is a dumb little shit.

"And when did Angelo and Tilly find out about him?"

"Right before my eighteenth birthday, but by then, it was too late."

"And your father isn't in jail?" I ask, astonished that he didn't unalive the man as soon as he found out about their affair.

"Rowdy isn't that much older than me, Asher. Stop being a prude."

"He's five years older, Tate. It's too old. When you were sixteen, he was twenty-one. And that's just…" I make a gagging sound. As much as I love women, there's no way in hell I would've been trolling high schools for girls when I wanted to get laid. "It's just wrong."

"But now, we're both in our twenties. The age gap is smaller."

"It doesn't matter what anything is now. It's about what it was when it started."

"Whatever," she mutters, clearly annoyed with me and my take on her situation.

"It doesn't matter now. What's done is done."

"Thank you." She smiles at me and starts to tap the side of her thumb against the countertop.

She looks relieved. I may say what's done is done, but I'm far from being done with the topic. If by some miracle Rowdy gets out of jail, there's no way in hell he's getting close to my little cousin again.

"So, why don't you tell me what the hell happened that has you hiding out down here."

Tate crumples forward, placing her head against her arm. "Ugh. It's so exhausting. I've gone over this again and again."

"Hey, shithead. You're going to keep going over it until we all know why we're putting ourselves at risk for your punk ass until Uncle James and Uncle Thomas figure out a solution to take the heat off you."

Her gaze narrows on me, and her top lip curls. "Sounds like you know enough already."

"Fuck it," I say, throwing up my hands, and start to stalk away.

But before I can get more than a few feet, Tate's hands are on me, stopping my forward motion. "Wait," she pleads. "I'll tell you."

I take a few steps back, stopping at the side of the desk. "Talk."

She drops her arms to her sides and leans back in the chair. "Rowdy was into some bad shit, but I never got involved. He got arrested, and for some crazy-ass reason, his brothers in the MC think I ratted on him. It wasn't me. It had to be someone else, but since they're coming up blank, they're pinning it on me and they're out for blood."

"Lovely."

"I just need to talk to Ranger, and he'll realize it wasn't me."

"Ranger?"

"The president of the club. He's sometimes a reasonable man."

"Sometimes?" I raise an eyebrow.

"You don't get to be the president by being a mediator and having great negotiation skills."

Gigi stalks into the customer waiting area, snapping off a pair of black protective gloves. "Is she telling you about Ranger?"

"Yep."

"What a shitshow," Gigi mumbles. "We'll be lucky if we all get out of this alive."

"The guys will handle it," I assure her. "They got you out of shit just as bad, if I remember correctly."

She snarls at me. "It was different."

"It was an MC."

"But still different, and they had some sort of fucked-up relationship with those guys from their days in the DEA."

"Can I have my phone back, please?" Tate asks Gigi, holding out her hand. "I need it."

"Nope. Your dad mailed it to me and said you could have it back after everything's done. Uncle Thomas and Uncle James said no too. You can't be trackable."

"I doubt Ranger's going to track my phone. The man doesn't even know how to text."

Gigi leans into Tate's space. "Babe, I'm going to say this one last time, and if you ask me again, I'm going to take a hammer to the bitch and break it into a million little pieces."

Tate's eyes grow wide as she leans back, trying to gain some personal space.

I stare in complete fascination, watching Gigi's badass side come out in force. It's rare that she shows that side, but when she does…it's something to behold.

"Ranger doesn't need to know how to text to track your ass through your phone's location. Men like him have guys on their payroll who can get them that information. There are dirty people everywhere. Stop acting like a dumb fucking kid with your head so far up your own ass you can almost see daylight coming from your own throat. You are not getting it back until we're all in the clear. Got it?"

Tate swallows before nodding slowly.

"Words, babe. I want to hear that you're getting what I'm saying and not going to ask me for it again."

"I got it. I won't ask again."

"Damn fucking right. I'm giving it to Uncle James and Uncle Thomas. You can ask them for it next time."

"No." Tate shakes her head quickly. "They're scary as fuck."

I chuckle, leaving them to hash out the rest of the conversation, but I know Gigi has it under control.

"Sounds like shit's going down out there," Pike says, peering up from his client's calf. "Been going on like this for the last hour since she got dropped off here straight from the airport."

"Who dropped her off here?"

"James and Thomas. They couldn't stick around but said they'd pick her up in a few hours to talk."

"I'm sure that'll go smoothly."

Pike laughs as he goes back to inking the guy's flesh. "I'd love to be in the room to hear her talking to them with that attitude."

"She used to be a sweet kid."

Lily pokes her head out of the piercing room. "Don't lie," she tells us. "She was a sweet kid when she was little, but nothing except attitude and trouble after that." As soon as she says the last word, she goes back into the room and closes the door.

"Tate's a lot like Gigi was when I met her," Pike says, smiling. "She was such a spitfire."

"She still is," I say to him as I walk over to my station and open the cabinet, getting out the supplies I'll need for my first client.

I'm halfway set up, still listening to Tate and her bullshit when my phone buzzes with a text from Olive.

> Olive: How late are you working tonight?

I stare at the phone and immediately know something is wrong. She made it clear that she wouldn't have time for me every night, and I was good with that. The fact that she wants to know when I'm going to be off tonight means she's coming over.

Me: What happened?

Olive: It's too much to type.

Me: Call me.

A few seconds later, my phone rings. I hit answer and wedge the phone between my shoulder and ear as I continue to work.

"What happened?"

Olive blows out a long, hard breath. "I came here to get my keys. It wasn't the same person I met with when I filled out the paperwork and put down my deposit."

"Okay…"

"They didn't turn in my paperwork and didn't deposit my check into the apartment's bank account. They took the money, Asher." Her voice cracks as she continues to explain. "My parents wrote a check to prepay the apartment for the entire year. They're going to lose their shit."

I don't even think before I say, "Don't tell them."

"How am I going to do that, Asher? I don't have the money to pay rent on top of my tuition. I don't have time for a job between my studies and the research program. I can maybe apply for another scholarship, but they're probably all gone by now. Fuck me."

I drop down into my chair, wondering if this is actually a bad thing or if fate has stepped in and is giving us a nudge to be together sooner. "Stay with me."

There's silence on the other end of the line.

"I have a spare bedroom you can set up as a study space, and we have different hours."

"That's too much."

"Too much what?" I ask her.

"Too much for you. You're used to being a bachelor and having your space."

"And you're not?"

There's more silence.

"At least until you see if you can get a scholarship or figure something else out. If you do, then you go wherever. If you don't, you have a safe place to stay."

But I want her to stay and hope nothing else works out. Maybe that's shitty of me, but I don't care. I want Olive with me. I am ready for that, having spent enough time apart.

"Okay," she whispers. "Temporarily, at least."

"Sure, sweetheart. For as long as you want or need. Come to the shop, and I'll give you the keys."

"Is it in the same spot?"

"Yep. You remember how to get here?"

"Of course. I used to press my face against the window, trying to catch a peek of someone getting a tattoo."

I smile at the thought of good girl Olive dying to be a little bad. "You want one?"

She laughs. "I don't know."

That's a yes in my book. "When you get one—"

"I'm not getting one."

"When you get one, I want to be the one to do it," I say, ignoring her. "No one else. Got me?"

"I got you," she says softly. "But I'm not getting one."

"We'll see."

"Whatever," she mutters. "I'll be there in thirty to get the keys or wait with you until you're done."

"I'll be here another three hours or so. The guy hasn't shown up yet."

"I'll wait for you at your house."

"I'll see you soon, sweetheart. Drive safe."

"Bye," she says, disconnecting the call.

Things are looking up. I'll savor every minute I have her under my roof, and I'll do everything in my power to keep her there.

CHAPTER 17
OLIVE

I PULL down my visor and flip open the mirror to check my makeup. I've cried more today than I have in years, and the evidence is all over my face. I reach into my purse, trying to find something to wipe away my smeared mascara, but I have nothing.

I wet my fingertips, dragging them across the black streaks on my cheeks, hoping it's enough to not be completely obvious that I've had tears streaming down my face for the last hour.

I wish I had a purse full of makeup to wipe away all the evidence, but I've never been that kind of girl.

I jump as someone knocks on the driver's side window. I place my hand on my chest, taking a deep breath. "Jesus," I mutter, hating that I'm on edge. I turn my head and smile as I see Gigi standing outside, waving at me.

"Open up," she says and holds up a bottle of

concealer along with a small washcloth. "I got you, boo."

It's like she was sent from heaven above to rescue me in a moment of cosmetic weakness. I roll down my window, wanting to leap through the opening to hug her.

"I heard what happened, and when I saw you through the window, I figured you could use this." She extends her hand to me, giving me the makeup and towel.

"You're the sweetest ever," I say to her, taking everything she has in her hands. "I could kiss you."

She laughs as she gazes down at me. "I don't think Asher would like that. I know I'm a better kisser than him."

I want to ask how she knows that, but I figure some secrets are better left buried. "Did he tell you?"

Her easy smile turns pained. "I hope you don't mind. We don't have any secrets here. And when you called him, we heard the conversation."

"It's okay," I whisper, but I'm a little embarrassed even though I shouldn't be. I didn't do anything wrong. People get swindled all the time, including me. "I figured as much."

"When we find the guy, I'll kick him straight in the balls for you," Gigi says as she places her hands on the window frame and leans closer. "He'll never walk right again or be able to bear children."

"You're so sweet, Gigi."

"No one fucks with my family and doesn't feel the sting of my steel-toed boots."

I blink, replaying what she just said. She called me *family*. I try to form words, try to come up with something to say, but I draw a blank because I'm reeling from what she said.

"ALFA will find them."

"ALFA?" I ask, buying myself time to get my mental shit together.

Gigi straightens and grabs her hair, pushing it behind her shoulders. "My uncles' investigation company. They can find anyone and anything. He can't hide forever."

"That's too much."

She shakes her head. "No, it's not. It's what they do, and when one of us is wronged, they always figure it out and set things straight."

"I don't—"

Gigi holds out her hand and shushes me. "Come on. Asher's waiting for you."

I cut the engine, instantly missing the air conditioning. The heat has been oppressive lately, and I hope, in time, I'll get better used to it. "Is this crazy?" I ask her as I climb out.

"What part?"

"Staying with Asher?"

Gigi laughs as she walks at my side toward the door. "No."

"Did you and Pike move in together this quick?"

Gigi chuckles. "Pike and I have a long and complicated history. Way too much for a short walk to the shop door."

"It's crazy. I know it's crazy."

"What else can you do?"

I shrug. "I don't know. Maybe my grandparents will let me live with them."

"Would you want that?"

I hate the thought of even asking, let alone moving in to their home. They're not the most loving, and I would assume they wouldn't make me feel welcome. "Not really."

Gigi stops and touches my arm. "Can I ask you something?"

I turn to face her, standing outside the shop on the walkway. "Sure."

"Do you love Asher?"

I stare at her, contemplating the question. "I've always loved Asher," I answer honestly. "But I don't know him that well now. I love the Asher from high school."

Gigi makes a gagging noise. "He was such an asshole back then. A cocky little motherfucker who thought his shit didn't stink and that he was God's gift to women."

"He wasn't that bad."

Gigi rolls her eyes. "He was awful, and if you loved him then, you have to love him now. He's a good man."

I nod. "I think he is. He seems to be."

"No seem about it. He is. Don't judge him from his past. People change, and if anyone has changed for the better, it's Asher."

"He's not a womanizer anymore?"

Gigi grimaces. "He hasn't been since he met you."

Well, that's something, except he was still a womanizer up until a few months ago. "What if I'm not enough for him?"

I'd be more than enough for most men, but Asher isn't just anyone. The man today can't be too far from the teenager of the past.

Gigi grabs my hand and squeezes. "You're more than enough. God," she breathes, "Pike was such a dick when I met him. The man was drowning in pussy, but that shit stopped when he met me. Men change, especially when they find what they've spent their life searching for."

"And that's me?"

She nods with the biggest smile. "Yep. It's you. When they find the one, it's like a switch is flipped, and there's never any going back. Stop questioning it and second-guessing your feelings or his and ride that wave for as long as you can. It'll be a wild ride."

"Is it that easy?" I ask.

She nods again and squeezes my hand. "Throw up your hands and let go."

The door to the shop opens, and Asher steps

outside. His gaze moves between Gigi and me. "Everything okay?"

I smile at Gigi before turning my gaze toward Asher. "Hey," I say softly. "We're good."

Gigi drops my hands and stalks toward Asher. When she's next to him, she bumps him with her hip. "You can thank me later," she tells him.

His eyebrows furrow as he looks at her in complete confusion. "What?"

"I'll tell you someday," she says to him and disappears into the shop, leaving us alone.

He opens his arms, and I can't stop myself from running into his embrace. "It'll be okay," he says in a soothing voice as he presses his lips to my hair. "I promise."

"I feel like a fool," I whisper into his soft T-shirt, tightening my arms around his middle. "I hate this feeling."

"You're not a fool. It happens to people all the time, Oli. At least you're not alone."

I haven't thought much about it since I found out I'd been swindled. I'm not alone. Sure, I've always had River, but my parents, grandparents, and the rest of my family have never been a great support system. So far, Asher and the Gallos have been more caring and helpful than anyone I share blood with.

I peer up at him, his arms still firmly around me. "What if…" My voice trails off.

I haven't allowed myself to really let Asher in. I've

been projecting my issues onto him. No one in my life has become close to me and stayed. What if we don't work out? Not only would I lose him, I'd lose his entire family. My life has been so empty for so long. I am used to it. It's my normal. But I can feel his family starting to weave their way into my world, and I want them there. I want to feel part of something.

Asher looks down at me with kindness in his eyes. "What if what, Oli?"

"What if we don't work out?"

"Again with this," he says softly. "I'm not who I used to be."

I shake my head, burying my face in his chest. "I don't want to be alone anymore," I admit, the words almost sticking in my throat. "If we get too comfortable, if I get too comfortable, and we fall apart, I'm not sure I could survive."

Asher places the side of his finger under my chin, forcing my gaze upward. "Have a little faith. I'm not going anywhere. You just came back into my life, and there's no way I'm letting you go without a fight. I want you here, and if I'm honest, I'm happy as shit that your apartment fell through."

I search his eyes, though I see nothing but sincerity. "Okay," I say softly, my voice barely audible even to myself.

"Now, do you want to come inside to hang out with everyone while I finish this tattoo, or do you want to head home now?"

Home. He called it home. Not *his place*, but home. And I'd be lying to myself if I didn't admit that it makes my heart beat a little faster and my belly do a few somersaults.

"I'll wait."

He smiles before kissing my lips. "Good. Everyone's waiting to see you."

"Great," I mumble, slightly embarrassed that I have to talk about what happened to his family.

"It'll be painless," he promises, staring into my eyes with such softness. He hooks his arm around my shoulder, pulling me toward the door.

I move with him, giving in to whatever is about to come. "I've got this," I say softly, giving myself a pep talk before we step into Inked.

Asher moves us toward the door and pulls away, placing his palm against the small of my back. A sense of relief washes over me as we step inside, and I'm blasted by the air conditioning.

A woman I've never met before is sitting behind the reception counter.

"Olive, this is my cousin Tate," Asher says, ticking his chin toward the woman. "And Tate, this is my girlfriend, Olive."

Those words sound so foreign coming from him. All the years I'd known him when we were younger, he never called anyone his girlfriend. Never. Not once. But it rolled off his tongue like it was the most natural thing in the world.

The woman pops off the seat, almost running in our direction. She opens her arms, throwing herself against me. I stagger back, barely keeping my balance as she wraps her arms around me.

"You're so freaking cute," she says, squeezing me absurdly hard. "I love you two together. You're perfect for my cousin."

"Thanks," I sputter, not sure what else to say.

She pulls back, grabbing at my arms to stop her backward momentum. "We're going to be the best of friends."

"She's suddenly nice," Asher says behind me.

Tate glares at him. "She's nice to me, so I'm nice to her."

"When was I mean to you?" he asks her.

Her hands leave my arms. "You've had an attitude with me since you walked in."

"Ridiculous," Asher mutters.

She raises her chin, looking every bit as defiant as I've seen the other people in this family be. She's a beautiful thing with her long, wavy brown hair, blue eyes, and flawless skin. "Is it?"

Asher steps up to my side, running his hand through his hair, making it a bigger mess than it already is. "Uh, yeah."

She wrinkles her perfect little nose. "You're all up in my shit about what happened."

"Your life is in danger."

She rolls her eyes at him. "Yeah, dummy. You

should be nicer in case I get popped the next time I step outside those doors."

I bite my lip, stopping myself from laughing at the two of them. I don't know if I should stay still or run for cover.

"I don't have time for this," Asher says, waving his hand at her. "I have a client waiting for me to finish." Asher leans over and kisses my cheek. "You want to sit back there with me?"

Tate shakes her head. "Olive and I are going to hang out here, right?"

I look from her to him, figuring why the hell not. "I'll be fine here."

He exhales and closes his eyes for a moment. "You sure?"

"Yeah, baby. I got this," I tell him.

"Baby?" Tate teases with a giggle. "It's so cute."

"Zip it," he tells her.

She makes a face, mocking him.

"Go." I give him a light shove, knowing this could go on for a long time. Someone has to be the adult in this situation, and it's me. "We'll be fine."

"Behave," he says, pointing at his cousin before he stalks off, leaving us in the front of the shop alone.

"Man, sometimes he's a royal pain in the ass," she says, shaking her head as she sinks back into the chair behind the desk. "How do you put up with him?" She pats the seat next to her. "Sit."

I place my purse on the floor and settle into the

chair next to her. The music in the shop is loud enough that I think we have some privacy, but not total. I've been told there's no such thing when it comes to this family. "So, what happened?" I ask her.

She hangs her head, and her shoulders sag. "I fucked up."

"Yeah?"

"Yeah." She brings her hands up to her face and drags her palms back and forth against her cheeks. "I fell in love with an asshole and got wrapped up in his shit."

"Damn," I mutter, but I knew as much. "Do you still love him?"

"Fuck no," she says immediately. "We broke up over a year ago."

My eyebrows rise. "Really?"

"Yeah," she whispers.

No one in the family seems to know that information. No one brought that up last night when they discussed the entire mess.

"Does anyone know that?"

She shakes her head. "I don't want to hear any *I told you so's* from anyone, especially this group." She pitches her thumb over her shoulder toward the work area of the shop. "They're judgy as fuck."

I nod. "They can be." I'm trying to play devil's advocate and get Tate to trust me. Hopefully no one's listening to our conversation, or else they'll throw me out before I've had a chance to really get in. “But don’t you think they need to know the whole story?”

She shakes her head, curling her top lip. “They’re on a need-to-know basis, and they don’t need to know.”

“What about the uncles?”

“They know. I’m not keeping shit from them.”

Well, at least we have that going for us. She is smart enough to at least confess that piece of information to the men who are trying to get her out of the mess. “Good. Good.”

“It’s why the club thinks I sold out Rowdy. They think I was petty enough to go to the Feds because I was hurt that a manwhore did what he does best and screwed anything with a vagina. I knew what he was. I’m not stupid. Rowdy was never faithful, and neither was I, honestly. But I’d never sell him out—or the guys in the club.”

“I thought you two were a thing…monogamous.”

She swipes her hand in the air, tips her head back, and barks out a laugh. “I just tell people that because it gets them all riled up. We were never exclusive, but he was one helluva fuck.” She smiles, staring out the front window. “Man was hung like a damn horse, and fuuuuck, he knew how to use that too. Don’t even get me started on his tongue work.”

My jaw drops. She talks like a biker and is way too out there and public about her sex life. “Why do you want to piss off your family?”

She shrugs. "I don't know. And it's not everyone. My parents know. It's mostly these guys." She points toward the back. "They expect it."

"They're good people."

She smiles sweetly. "They're the best. Well, besides my family in Chicago."

"I'm not sure there's a bad Gallo in the world."

"You haven't met my grandfather. It's debatable if he's good or not." She laughs. "Even my grandma isn't sure sometimes."

"He sounds interesting."

"You have no idea." She places a hand on her stomach. "I'm starving."

"Me too." With all the bullshit of the day, I've barely eaten and am starting to feel a bit light-headed.

"We should grab something from the sub shop a few doors down."

I chew on the inside of my lip, wanting to say yes, but knowing she's probably not allowed to go anywhere.

"I'll run back there and ask," she says, jumping up from the chair before I tell her I'll do it instead.

While she goes to the back, I take a moment to check my phone. There's only one missed text message from my brother.

> River: I took a few days off work. I'm going to come and make sure you're settled.

I stare at the phone, blinking. What in the world? My brother has never come to make sure I'm settled. He's never given a damn if I needed help or if I'm safe. We're close, but we lead different lives, and he's always given me space…until now.

Me: No. I'm good. Just about settled in.

I haven't called him to tell him what happened. He's a big mouth and will run right to my parents and tell them I was ripped off.

River: I miss the area and want to catch up with some old friends.

He's a liar. My brother hasn't missed a single person from here. He never bothered to reach out to anyone, and when he has talked about it here, it's always with an acrid attitude.

Me: Don't lie to me. Why are you really coming here?

River: Can't a brother visit his sister?

My lips twist into a frown. I wish I had a brother who was as close to me as the Gallos are to one another.

Me: Don't start any shit.

River: Do I ever?

That text is followed by a winky face.

"Ready," Tate says, stalking back into the customer waiting area from the back. "We got the all clear."

"Oh. Okay," I tell her, grabbing my purse off the floor and hustling to catch up with her before she makes it to the door. My stomach growls as soon as we're outside, and I'm hit with the smell of pepperoni and melting cheese. "I'm getting a cheesesteak."

"You need to visit me in Chicago. You'd love an Italian beef," she says and peers over her shoulder at me. Her eyes shift to the left and then widen.

CHAPTER 18
ASHER

"WHAT IN THE..."

Gigi walks out from the rear of the shop and runs right into my back. "What's wrong?" She steps out from behind me and gazes around the waiting room. "Where are they?"

"Fuckin' Tate, man." I ball my hands into fists and take a deep breath. There's no way I lost her already. Uncle James and Uncle Thomas will rip me a new asshole. "Does she have any sense of self-preservation?"

Gigi shakes her head. "Obviously not."

I stalk toward the door, a feeling of dread coming over me. "They better be safe or else…"

Gigi touches my arm. "Breathe, cousin. I'm sure they're fine. They probably went next door for something to eat."

I grunt my displeasure. “Tate knows better than to wander off without saying anything.”

“She does, but she obviously doesn’t give a fuck,” Gigi says as she drops her hand. “Don’t be too mean.”

I laugh at the seriousness on my cousin’s face. “Tate and I are going to have a chat.”

Gigi glances up at the ceiling and sighs. “Please don’t lose your cool.”

“I don’t have time for this shit,” I say as I punch open the front door to the shop and become momentarily blinded by the late-afternoon sun.

It’s only a few short steps to the sub shop, and I press my forehead to the glass, placing my hands on the sides of my face to block out the light.

“Little shit,” I mutter, catching sight of Tate as she stops laughing to take a bite of a sandwich.

Don’t lose your cool. Be calm. Be cool. Breathe, Asher.

I pull open the door, stalking into the sub shop.

“Hey, man,” Cliff, the guy behind the counter, says, giving me a chin lift.

Tate’s eyes come immediately to me, and she stops chewing as her face drains of all color.

At least she has enough sense to be scared. If I didn’t know better, I’d question her smarts after taking off from the shop when she knows damn well that people are out to get her.

I march to the table and lean over, placing my knuckles on top. “What in the hell are you doing?” I grit out, speaking slowly and deeply.

She leans back, trying to escape my glare. "I was…hungry."

Olive's hand touches my forearm. "We're safe."

I ignore her, knowing they're safe, but also knowing things could be very different. "You know better, Tate. You're always pulling shit, not caring who gets wrapped up in your crazy, bullshit life. We're all putting our necks on the line for you, and this is how you pay us back? What in the fuck is wrong with you?"

Tate's bottom lip quivers, the first real sign of remorse or fear she's shown since she was dropped off in our care. "I'm sorry… I…didn't…" Her eyes are wide when she speaks, and they're pinned on me.

"Think?" I narrow my eyes more, leaning a little closer so she can hear me but the other people sitting around us don't. "You didn't fucking think, Tate. What if it wasn't me coming in here, but one of the assholes from the club, looking to snatch you. Everyone in here could be dead, including you."

"Enough," Olive whispers, squeezing my arm. "We'll go. Stop making a scene."

I turn my head slowly, gazing at my girl. "It's not your fault. Tate knew what she was doing and how dangerous it was. She didn't give any shits, Oli. You could've—"

"But I didn't. I knew too, Ash, and I still came with her. It's better than her going alone. Now, let's go. We'll finish eating at the shop, and you and I can finish this conversation at home later." She pulls her hand away, and I instantly snap out of it.

Those words—at home later—strike me right in the gut. I like how they sound coming from her lips. The heat in my blood subsides enough for me to straighten and take a deep breath. "Let's go," I mutter, finally looking around the small sub shop, seeing every pair of eyes on us.

Tate scrambles to her feet, her hair flying wild with her speed. "I'm sorry," she says again, clutching her half-wrapped sandwich and soft drink in her hands.

Olive gives me a half smile. "I was stupid."

I shake my head, wishing I could've held my temper. "You were not. Tate knew, and she didn't care."

"She's young."

I wait for Olive to walk in front of me and follow behind the two girls, my eyes scanning the parking lot as we walk back toward Inked. "So are we. There's a difference between uncaring and young. She didn't care if she put your life in danger or her own."

"She's just a bit wild."

I stop as Tate walks into the shop, and Olive stops too. "Wild? You think she's only wild?" I throw my arm out toward the shop, waving my hand. "She's careless and selfish too."

Olive steps back toward me with a softness on her face. "I'm sure there was a time you were careless and selfish too. The boy I knew in high school was both of those things all the time."

I cross my arms, hating that she isn't wrong. "I grew up."

"She will too, Ash. Let it go."

I grab Olive and pull her against me until she's tucked under my chin. "I was an asshole when I was younger, but I never put anyone's life at risk, Oli, and neither did you."

Olive's body is warm, pressed against mine, as she wraps her arms around my middle, holding herself tighter to me. "Cut her a little slack, Ash. It'll all work out."

"Okay," I breathe out, trying to let go of the sense of panic I felt when they were missing from the waiting room. "I'll cut her a little slack, but not enough that she can hang herself. Self-preservation clearly isn't her strong suit."

Olive's body shakes in my arms. "It's genetic."

I pull my head back far enough to stare into her eyes. "I never had a death wish, babe."

Olive raises an eyebrow. "I remember some pretty stupid shit you did that could've ended with you in the ground."

I sigh again, hating that she's right. "You want the key to head over to the house?"

She shakes her head before placing it back against my chest. "No. I'll wait for you and keep Tate company so she doesn't wander off again."

I kiss her hair, wondering what I did to get so damn lucky. "Whatever you want."

"Exactly," she mutters into my T-shirt. "I want to stick around and see your uncles too."

"They're not that exciting."

"I think I met them a long time ago when we were younger, but from what I remember, they were, indeed, very exciting."

I grunt. "You thought they were hot, didn't you?" I make a gagging noise. "They were old."

"They were handsome and big."

"I'm handsome and big," I tease her.

She peers up at me and smiles. "I know," she says and winks.

I chuckle and shake my head. "You're ridiculous."

"I know," she says as she releases her grip around my waist and pulls me toward the door. "Don't you have a client?"

"He needed a few minutes."

"It's been longer than that."

I smile at her, wishing we could leave now. "Babe, trust me, he's not leaving with partial ink."

Olive doesn't let up, pulling me toward the door. "The sooner you start, the sooner we can go home."

If I didn't have the motivation before, I do now. "I'll make it quick."

She stops as her hand touches the handle. "You will not. Do a good job. I'm going to enjoy some time with your cousins."

"They're not that fun."

She giggles. "Maybe not to you, but they are to me."

"Okay. Okay," I say, opening the door for her.

When we step inside, Tate's in a chair across the room and as far away from Gigi as she can be. Her head's down, and she's fidgeting with her fingers.

"I've got her," Olive says and rushes to Tate's side.

"Don't worry about it, Tate. It's forgotten."

Tate lifts her head, her eyes swimming with tears. "I'm in so much trouble, Olive."

Olive gazes at me across the room and ticks her head toward the back. It's my cue to go, and I do just that.

"This is going to be worse than I thought," Lily says to Trace. "I don't know why I thought she maybe grew up a little bit."

"Ready?" I ask my client.

"Do your worst," he says, placing his noise-canceling headphones back on his ears.

I snap on a new pair of gloves and get back to work, listening to my cousins as they bitch about Tate.

"My dad will handle her," Trace says as he scrolls through his phone. "They'll fix shit."

"Before or after she gets her ass killed?" Rebel asks with her arms crossed as she leans against Rocco's station. "Because right now, it's not looking good."

Rocco pulls Rebel in front of him, placing his

hands on her hips. "She isn't going to die, Reb. She's a Gallo."

Rebel mutters under her breath. "You all don't always make the best decisions."

"We're all still breathing," he tells her.

"It's a freaking miracle," Rebel teases, tangling her fingers in my cousin's hair. "You've all been searching for the most asinine ways to die for a long time."

"We're just lucky," Carmello tells her as he wipes down the chair his previous client sat in. "Always have been, always will be."

"But does Tate have the same luck?" Rebel asks Carm.

"Time will tell, but since she has our blood, I'd say yes," Carmello replies.

"Dumbest shit I've ever heard," I mumble, earning me a wicked glare from my cousins.

"He's right," Lily says, always the sensible and sane one of the group. "None of us is immune to bad shit. If Tate isn't careful, she's not going to make it back home."

Lily tosses a cleaning rag over her shoulder before dropping into an empty chair. "It's our job to guide her."

I glance up at Lily. "Good luck with that."

Lily gives me a shitty smirk. "I'm sure she won't wander off for another sub sandwich after you no doubt laid into her pretty hard."

I straighten and lean back, stretching. "I didn't lay into her pretty hard. I barely scratched the surface."

Lily crosses her arms, tilting her head to the side like she doesn't believe a word coming out of my mouth. "Then why is she in tears?"

I shrug. "Hell if I know. Probably girl shit."

"Girl shit?" Lily chuckles. "You're a moron. I still can't believe you suckered Olive into being your girlfriend. I thought she was smarter than that."

"Magic cock, cousin. Magic cock."

Lily gags and throws up her arms. "I don't have time for this. I have a client coming."

I snicker as she stalks away. That'll serve her right for talking shit about me and how hard I laid into Tate. She knew I was pissed, but I didn't go off on her, and I'm wondering if I made the right call.

Only time will tell if Tate keeps her ass alive and comes out of this entire ordeal without a scratch along with the rest of us.

CHAPTER 19
OLIVE

"I HOPE you don't mind the mess," he says, and I turn my head to gawk at him.

"What?"

"The mess." He motions toward a single speck of sand on the light hardwood. "I went onto the beach earlier and tracked some in."

I imagine living so close to the beach, it's a constant issue, but one I'd be willing to live with to have this view. "I think I can deal with it."

Asher steps into my line of sight, blocking the view. "Now, do you want to sleep in my room or your own?"

I stare up at him, blinking. "My own…"

He nods. "I understand. It's all so new. I'll carry your stuff into your room."

I shake my head. "No. I mean, you'd give me an entire room?"

Asher's smile is easy and kind. "Oli, you can have the whole damn house. Whatever you want. I thought we could turn the spare room into a study for you, but then we'd have to share a room and a bed."

My heart swells inside my chest. No one's ever been so kind to me. I'm not sure if anyone in my entire family has ever been this nice to me. Without thinking for another second, I jump up as he snakes his arms around me, and I wrap my legs around his middle. I pepper his face with kisses, not knowing how else to show him how much I appreciate everything. "You're too good to me, Asher Gallo. Too good," I whisper into his skin as his five-o'clock shadow brushes against my lips.

He stalks across the room, palming my ass in his hands.

I squeal in delight as he carries me down the hallway, having missed the feel of his lips against my body.

I reach down, pulling off my shirt before my body hits the bed. I'm not about to waste a moment. Asher bends over, grabbing my shorts and underwear, and removes them in one dizzying motion.

"Now you," I say, motioning to his pants as I lie back on the bed, staring at him. "Take it all off."

His smirk is irresistible as he gazes down at me with hunger in his eyes. "I thought you'd never ask." He bends over again, taking his pants with him before he kicks them to the side.

My eyes slowly trail down his body when he stands, finding his cock hard and ready. I'm mesmerized as he pulls off his shirt, giving me the full view of himself.

I prop myself up on my elbows, soaking him in. "Damn. You're so pretty. Too pretty."

He laughs as he slides into the bed, nestling his torso between my legs. "I'm not pretty, Oli. That's you, baby," he whispers as he hovers over me. "The prettiest girl I've ever seen."

The compliment is great, but I know he's lying. But the way he looks at me makes me believe every word he's saying.

"Shut up and kiss me," I whisper as I slide my hands over his back, scraping the skin softly with my fingernails.

He rests his full weight against me, pressing his middle to mine. His lips take my mouth, stealing my moan before it has a chance to escape my lips.

He guides his cock to my opening, slowly pushing inside…filling me. There is a delicious bite of pain as my body adjusts to his size.

"Relax, baby," Asher whispers, staying still as if he can read my mind. "We'll go slower this time."

I flatten my palms against his back, pulling him tighter against my chest. "Make love to me, Asher," I say softly in his ear.

He moans before starting to move again, thrusting

into me over and over until we both fall over the edge, finding our pleasure.

CHAPTER 20
ASHER

"THIS IS JUST..."

I squeeze her hand, letting her know I understand when I don't. I've always had a big family, and Sunday dinner—or hell, any family occasion—warrants a small army to gather together to talk and eat. "Are you okay?"

Olive swallows and turns her gaze toward me. "Never better. It's different from your grandmother's house. I know all the faces here… Well, almost all of them."

"There're a few relative newbies who married into the family."

"So, Olive," Gigi says, rocking back and forth in the patio chair. "When you moved away, did you like your new school?"

Olive shakes her head. "It was awful. I was depressed for a long time about moving."

I squeeze her hand again, trying to imagine what it would've been like to move away from everyone and everything I'd known. "I can't imagine."

"At least I only had junior and senior year left. As soon as I could get out of there, I did."

"That sucks," Gigi mutters. "I can't even imagine."

"This isn't a small town, but where my parents moved us to certainly was, and cliques were established long before I got there. It was a lonely few years."

"Why didn't you stay in touch with us?" Tamara asks, always so direct.

Olive shrugs one shoulder. "It was too depressing."

"I get that," Lily says.

"If you've never moved, it's hard to understand the feeling of knowing nothing will ever be the same," Rebel adds. "It's an awful thing to deal with when you're a kid and have no power to change anything."

"Yeah," Olive whispers.

"But you're back now," I say, wanting to alter the mood of the conversation. "And I'm not letting you go again."

Olive's eyes meet mine, and a smile slides across her face. "Promise?"

I lift her hand to my lips. "Promise."

"Aww," Tamara says.

"Who would've thought Asher would be all

wrapped up in a woman?" Mammoth says with his arm slung around the back of my sister's chair.

"Did you ever think you'd be pussy-whipped?" I ask him with my chin raised.

He smirks, running his fingers across the top of my sister's shoulder. "I hoped, but I didn't think it would be this freaking great."

"Unkie Ash," a little voice says from the patio.

I turn my head, spotting Riley. "What's up, baby girl?"

She smiles and bounces toward me, leaping into my lap. "Are we going to make sundaes again?"

I wrap my arms around her, wishing I could keep her this little forever. "Whatever you want, Ri."

She reaches up, placing her soft little hands on my cheeks. "With whipped cream?"

I nod.

She leans forward, almost toppling into me, but I catch her before she smacks her head on my nose. "And hot fudge?" she whispers.

"You can have everything on it, but does Nonna have hot fudge or did we eat it all last week?"

Her shoulders sag forward. "Oh. Crap."

"Why don't you ask Gram? I bet she got some for you," Mammoth tells her.

"I don't know if she should have all that sugar," Tamara says. "She'll be a beast to put to sleep tonight."

"She'll be okay," Mammoth says.

Tamara turns her entire body, leaning back into the armrest, and stares at her husband. "Oh really? Are you going to do it, then?"

"Sure," he says smugly. "It won't be that hard."

Tamara laughs as she shakes her head. "I'm going to take pleasure in watching your misery."

"Unkie Ash," Riley says, still perched on my lap. "Do we have to wait until after dinner?"

I look down at her and smile. She's relentless and has the biggest sweet tooth out of everyone in the family. "Yeah, baby. Gram would be so sad if we spoiled our dinners."

"I don't want basta."

"Why?" I tap her nose as she giggles.

"Pasta is so tasty covered in all that sauce."

"Lemme down," she says, kicking her feet until I put her feet on the cement. "I'm going to talk to Nonna." She marches off like a girl on a mission.

"You're good with her," Olive says, placing her hand on my arm.

"I love that tiny squirt. She has me wrapped around her little finger."

Riley's had my heart since the day she was born. I never thought much about having kids of my own until my niece and nephew were born. Tamara didn't seem like the motherly type, but she embraced the role and thrived.

"Do you want kids?" Olive asks.

Before Riley and Jackson were born, I would've

said no, but now…

"Absolutely."

"How many?"

I don't even have to think about my answer because it's something I've thought about before. "At least two. Anything more is a bonus."

"Bonus kids?" She smiles. "So, like, eight is okay?"

My eyes widen as panic starts to set in. "No. No. No. Not eight. That's way too many."

Olive pats my hand as she relaxes deeper into the chair. "Four?"

I nod, imagining four little ones running around the house, and they all look like Olive. "Four is perfect."

"Would you be a stay-at-home dad?"

Tamara snorts. "I could picture Asher as Mr. Mom."

"He'd be great, wouldn't he?" Olive asks Tamara, both teasing me at this point.

"No shade at a dude who wants to stay home with his kids, but that life isn't for me."

"Hey," Tate says as she walks outside, tucking a lock of her dark hair before her ear. "Can I join you guys?"

Lily pulls an empty chair closer to where we're sitting. "Of course, silly."

"What's up, kid?" Gigi asks her, always reminding everyone that she's the oldest one of the group. "Are they making you crazy in there?"

"No. I love them, even if they get a little nosy."

Luna snorts. "Only a little nosy?"

"That's the understatement of the year," Rosie adds. "Especially Aunt Fran. She's the worst."

"She has more secrets than the Vatican's basement," Carmello blurts out, and I almost fall off my chair from the funniness of the statement.

"Dude," Nevin says as he smacks Carm's arm. "Don't talk shit about Fran. She's my favorite little shit-stirrer in this family."

"She's a lot like my grandpa," Tate says and turns her head to stare out across the backyard to where some of the younger ones are playing on a swing set.

"How are Uncle Santino and Aunt Betty?" Trace asks.

"The same as always, but maybe with a bit more spice."

"Spice?" Rosie asks with a raised eyebrow.

"Yeah, they…"

Rosie sticks out her hand. "I don't want to know."

"No, it's not like that," Tate giggles. "They fight like cats and dogs sometimes. Grandpa causes a lot of trouble, and Grandma isn't having it."

"What do they think about what's happening with you?" Gigi asks, going straight for the grandparent guilt.

Tate's shoulders fall forward as she glances down at her lap. "She's not happy."

I know the look on her face. I've had it a few times

in my life. It's the way only a grandmother's disappointment can weigh on your soul.

"She'll be okay once this is over," Tamara tells Tate, trying to make her feel better.

"Maybe," Tate mumbles, setting her hands in her lap, and starts to fidget. "Depends on if the club finds me before things can get straightened out."

"They won't find you," Mammoth says.

"We'll make sure of it," Pike adds.

"How do you know?" Tate asks, glancing toward them.

"We just do," Mammoth states.

Mammoth and Pike have the most knowledge about MCs, both having been part of that world and possessing a knowledge base no one else here has.

Pike leans forward, placing his elbows on his knees. The man oozes cool, and so does Mammoth, but Pike's is more natural. "Our friends are on it."

"Your friends?" Tate swallows, her eyes wide.

Pike nods as he cracks his neck. "We have contacts all over the state who know that world. Shit will get straightened out quicker than you think, and if it doesn't, we have eyes everywhere."

"And my dad and Uncle James will make sure shit gets settled," Nick says.

"I hope so," Tate whispers.

"How long were you and Rowdy together?" Nick asks.

"Well, um…" Tate mumbles before her voice dies.

"Tell them," Olive says, making me turn my gaze toward her.

What don't I know? Hell, what doesn't everyone around this table not know, but somehow, Olive does? Maybe their lunch together was more useful than I could've ever imagined.

"What?" Lily says, scooting her chair a little closer to the table. "Tell us."

"Oh boy," Tamara mumbles. "This ought to be good."

"It's okay," Olive says to Tate.

"We were never an exclusive couple. It was only sex and fun."

"Fucking insane," I whisper, wrapping my hand around the armrest of the patio chair.

Olive gives me a pleading look, and I shut the hell up, not wanting to piss her off.

"We called it quits over a year ago. I was sick of not being important in his life, and I didn't want to share him anymore. He was unwilling to be a one-woman man, and I was unwilling to be just another one of his girls. It was a mutual decision. I was ready to move on. I should've done it a long time ago."

"Then why does the club think it was you who sold him out?" Rosie asks.

"They thought I was hurt and lashed out. In their minds, women aren't rational creatures."

"Men," Luna groans. "Dumb as hell."

"Rowdy will always have a special place in my heart. He's not a bad guy."

I roll my eyes. He's not a good guy, and I don't care what she says. She'll never convince me otherwise.

"I haven't even spoken to Rowdy in months, but the club doesn't know that. They think I'm the only one who could've possibly flipped on him, but I'm not a narc. His cock was good, but not that damn special. None of them are."

"Preach," Tamara says with a nod.

"Princess, you say otherwise when we're alone," Mammoth says, smirking at my sister.

Tamara waves him away. "We need to feed the male ego sometimes."

"Any idea who could've talked?" Pike asks Tate.

"Rowdy wasn't much of a talker, and I can't imagine him being any different with any other women in his life."

"Men do dumb shit for pussy," Rocco says.

"Truer words have never been spoken," Rebel, his wife, agrees.

"All I know is it wasn't me."

Gigi places her hand on Tate's shoulder. "Don't worry. It'll all work out."

"I hope so. I enjoy being alive," Tate says softly.

And I wonder if we'll all make it out of this experience still breathing, or if my cousin's fuck boy will land one of us six feet underground.

CHAPTER 21
OLIVE

"HOW'S YOUR NEW PLACE?" my mom asks during her weekly phone call to make sure I'm alive.

Beyond that, my mother doesn't have much of a motherly side. She loves babies, but once my brother and I were able to do things on our own, she wiped her hands of us.

I glance around Asher's house, hating that I need to lie, but knowing it's necessary. "It's nice."

"All settled?"

"Yes."

"Good."

There's a long silence, neither one of us having much to say to the other.

"Anything else?" she asks.

"No."

"Glad to be back in Tampa?"

"Yes. It's been nice."

"Find any of your old friends?"

"A few," I tell her, leaving out about the Gallos.

"Good. Good. Well, be safe and call me next weekend."

"Anything you want to talk about?" I ask her, wishing I had a speck of the relationship with my mom that Asher and his cousins have with theirs. "Are you okay? Anything new?"

"I've been busy in the garden, and your father has been tinkering on his boat. Other that than, nothing."

His boat is an old wooden boat that hasn't run in thirty years. He's spent the last ten restoring it but has barely made a dent in it because he constantly gets sidetracked.

"Well, I have to run," she says. "I need to water."

"Okay. Bye, Mom."

"Bye, Olive," she replies and hangs up.

No I love you.

No take care.

No nothing.

Just a click.

There's a click because my parents still have a landline and refuse to give anyone their cell phone numbers. Their only purpose is for them to make phone calls if they have an emergency outside the house.

I set my phone on the armrest next to me as I curl my feet under my bottom, nuzzling my body into the couch. The ocean's turbulent today, and the clouds are shifting from white to gray. A storm is brewing, the typical evening ones we experience almost daily in Florida.

When I moved away, I missed the torrential rain and thunder that shook the house like clockwork every afternoon.

The couch dips at my side as Asher sits down. "What's wrong?"

"Nothing." I turn to him and smile before moving my gaze back to the beach. "I'm good."

"Who was on the phone?"

"My mom."

"Ah," he says. "That's why your mood changed faster than the weather outside."

"Do you remember her?"

"I do. I only met her a few times, but she's…"

"I know. She's the same. She's about as warm as a block of granite. I always accepted it. I knew what she was, and I was okay with it. I had River, at least. But being around your family, watching the warmth and love…" I sigh, resting my head against my palm. "It makes it hard for me to come to terms with realizing it'll never be anything more."

"You have us," he says and scoots closer to me. He extends his arm, resting it against my leg. "I know it's not the same, but it's better than nothing. And you still have River."

"He's been more of a pain in the ass than normal lately."

River has always had my back, but this is the first time he's ever come out against something I'm doing. And by something I'm doing, I mean Asher.

River has a distaste for him, but not the typical kind he had for previous men in my life. There's something more there that River hasn't told me about, and I'm not sure if he'll ever be able to move beyond it.

"He hates me," Asher says, surprising me.

I shift on the couch to face him. "Why?"

Asher glances down for a moment, rubbing his hands on his jeans. "Do you remember Samantha Maroni?"

I nod, ignoring the heat in my belly at the mention of her name. "Sadly, I do."

Asher grimaces as he brings his gaze back to mine. "I slept with her."

Somehow, I don't gag. I never liked Samantha. She was mean to everyone with a set of boobs, even me when she was dating my brother. Instead of sucking up to me like his other girlfriends, Samantha made sure I knew she hated me. "This is my shocked face." I point at my impassive look. Asher slept with as many, if not more, women as my brother did. The knowledge that Samantha's on his list isn't surprising at all.

Asher gives me a sad smile. "I'm not proud of it… of who I was…how I was."

"And how was that?"

"A horny teenage moron."

I snort. "Why does River hate you about Samantha? Did it happen before or after he dated her?"

"During."

I suck in a breath through my teeth. "Damn."

Asher nods slowly and exhales. "It's why they ended."

Now all my brother's anger toward Asher makes sense. Samantha and River only dated for a short time, but River was crazy about her. I knew it wouldn't last. Samantha wasn't about monogamy, and their relationship was destined to be short-lived, even if Asher hadn't slept with her.

"He needs to get over it. It's not like they were going to walk down the aisle someday. Samantha was never going to be his wife. You were a dumb kid, as were Samantha and River."

"You're not mad at me?" he whispers, looking embarrassed and worried about what he just admitted.

I shake my head. "It happened a decade ago. You were a kid, and Samantha had a role to play in it too. Whatever happened is between you and my brother.

I'm not going to judge you for something you did before you even had pubic hair."

"Babe, I had pubic hair. I wasn't a kid."

"You were a kid, and that person is nothing like the man you are today, is he?"

Asher grabs my hand, clasping it gently. "I'm nothing like that stupid teenager today, Olive. Nothing."

I stare into his eyes, knowing every word of what he's saying is sincere. "I know. We all change over time, Asher. We grow and learn. Men tend to do it a little slower than women, but you eventually get there."

"I can't argue with that. I've seen it with my own eyes with my cousins."

"But if you ever change your mind and realize this life isn't for you, tell me. I'll go before you have a chance to rip my heart out."

It guts me to say those words. We've barely begun, but this feels different from the other relationships I'd been in. I've known Asher most of my life, and if things ended, I'd feel an emptiness that would rival when my parents moved us away.

Asher moves quickly, sliding his arms underneath my legs and lifting me in the air. I'm like a feather in his grasp as he shifts me around until my back is flush against his front. He places his chin on my shoulder, his mouth next to my ear. "You'd let me go without a fight?"

"Yes," I say, knowing I wouldn't fight for something the other person didn't really want. I wouldn't force a man to be with me. It could only end in a bigger disaster and more heartache.

"I'd fight for you," he whispers against my ear.

"I'm not going anywhere," I promise him.

He tightens his arms around my middle as he splays his hands against my stomach. "You say that now, Olive, but a smart woman like you may get sick of a regular guy like me with mild intelligence."

"You're smart, Asher. Don't sell yourself short. You run an entire business."

"Not by myself."

"You're still smart, though. I mean…you waited for me, right?" I turn my head, our faces so close to each other I can feel his warm breath caressing my skin.

"I don't think my heart ever fell in love with anyone because it knew you were out there, and it was waiting for you to come back."

My vision begins to blur with those words. "Why are you so sweet?"

"I'm just being me, Oli. I'm a reformed asshole, but that man is long gone."

"I don't know what I did to get so lucky to find you again."

"Fate, baby. Fate. We were meant to be," I tell him, staring into his eyes.

His gaze darkens as he leans over, kissing my

mouth gently. I grip his T-shirt, curling my fingers into the soft fabric to ground myself.

It is still hard for me to believe I am with Asher. And not just messing around, having a fling. We are turning into something more than I ever could've dreamed.

CHAPTER 22
ASHER

"DO we need to set ground rules?" I ask Tate as she settles onto the couch in my living room.

Her lips twist, and her attitude bubbles to the top. "No," she snaps.

"We'll be fine," Olive says, grabbing on to my arm.

Olive will be fine, but Tate's bound to find trouble wherever she can. It's the gift most women in this family have somehow genetically inherited.

I glance down at Olive as she places the side of her head against my bicep. "You're in charge. Don't take any shit."

"I am an adult," Tate says, picking at her long, black-painted fingernails. "I'm capable of taking care of myself."

"You're here, aren't you?"

"It's because someone is trying to murder me, not

because I'm not a grown-ass woman. I'm not the first woman in this family to be in this kind of danger."

"I know," I grumble. "You're all a magnet for it."

"It's our Gallo gift," she says flippantly like it's not a big deal that there is a group of men searching for her, wanting to slit her throat.

"Don't go outside too much, and if you do, keep it brief." I raise an eyebrow, waiting for the pushback.

"Okay," she says, sounding a bit defeated.

"We'll stay in and binge something on television," Olive reassures me. "Don't worry."

I can't help but worry about Olive's safety. Tate's too, but she looks for trouble, while Olive has always done her best to keep her nose clean. But Tate…Tate will sniff it out because she's careless and thinks she'll always come out unscathed.

"What do you need before I go?"

Tate lifts her legs onto the couch, stretching out. "Popcorn."

"Sweet Jesus," I mutter under my breath. "Why do you always have to be such a jagoff?"

Tate snorts. "You make it too easy."

"I'll get whatever she needs," Olive says, giving my arm a squeeze. "Go. I don't want you to be late and keep a client waiting."

I lean forward, pressing my lips to Olive's soft mouth. "Are you sure?"

"Yes. I'll text you if we need anything. Maybe I'll order us a pizza."

Tate grunts from her perch on the couch. "They have the worst pizza down here. We'll order wings or something."

"Whatever," I grumble. "She tries anything, call me or call my uncles. You have their numbers."

"Go," Tate blurts out. "I promise to behave."

Do I believe her promise? Not in the slightest, but I trust Olive and her ability to keep shit under control. Not Tate, though. You can't control the uncontrollable. Keeping Tate in line is like herding cats.

"Go," Olive says again, pushing me toward the door. "I'll text you every hour to let you know we're safe."

"Gross," Tate mutters. "That's a little over the top. Don't you think?"

"It's not," I say, but I don't look at Tate when I say the words. My gaze is pinned on Olive as she steps around to my front. "Keep me posted. I love you."

A moment of silence stretches between us like we're in an echo chamber and could hear a pin drop in the room. I've never said that to anyone besides family before. And this time, it rolled off my tongue like it was something I said every day. It was so natural and normal that I almost didn't realize I said it except that Olive's eyes widened for a brief second.

"I love you too," Olive says back to me before she presses her body against me. "See you later."

"Later," I say, barely getting the words out as my mouth touches hers.

"Later," she breathes and pulls away from me.

That's not the way I wanted to say that to her the first time. It felt so cold and impersonal while I was in the middle of giving Tate shit about being here. Damn. I'll have to make it up to Olive. Do something to make it special. She deserves as much.

I grab my keys and stalk out of the house, pissed off at myself and trying to think of a way to get it right the next time.

"How was Tate at your place?" I ask Gigi as I settle into my chair at the shop.

"Fine. Fine. She's changed a lot."

My forehead crinkles as I gawk at Gigi. "For real?"

Gigi nods as she takes a bite from a bagel half. "Yeah, man. It's crazy. You'll see," she says while chewing the bread and cream cheese.

"I don't see it."

Gigi wipes her lips with the back of her hand. "Dude, you need to drop the attitude when it comes to her. She's family, and she was a kid. She's a woman now. As soon as you give her attitude, she gives it right back in spades. She's not an idiot, Asher. She's scared right now, and she doesn't know how to deal with that. You constantly attacking her or treating her like an idiot doesn't help anything."

"She doesn't seem afraid."

Gigi shakes her head, frowning. "Men. All clueless."

"What?"

"She doesn't want to look weak. Scared isn't an easy emotion for many of us. Can't you understand that?" Gigi takes another bite, this time a bigger one, but keeps her eyes on me.

I've rarely been scared in my life. It's happened so few times, I can't even think of a specific moment when I've felt true fear. Sure, there have been times I've done dumb shit that could've gotten me killed, but the thought of my mortality never entered into my mind while I was doing them.

I run my hand back and forth over my hair, blowing out a long, deep breath. "I can't. Never been there."

She groans as she swallows the mouthful of bagel. "I've been there, and it sucks. It must be nice to go through life without ever being scared."

"I guess."

"When Pike's father was after us and shit was going on with the MC, I was terrified. I was probably a brat at the time too because I was kind of helpless and only had the ability to be angry."

Stone walks in, looks at Gigi and then at me. "Fuck. This looks intense."

I laugh. "You ever been scared?"

"Of what?" he asks, looking confused.

"Anything," I tell him, leaning back in my chair as I cross my arms.

He drops into his chair, scrubbing his hand across his chin. "Like scared, or pissing-my-pants afraid?"

"What's your idea of scared?" I ask as Gigi continues to eat her bagel, staring at us like we're idiots, which we probably are.

"A haunted house."

"Morons," Gigi mutters under her breath between bites. "Both of them."

"Zip it," I snap in her direction before turning back to Stone. "Have you ever been afraid for your life?"

Stone immediately shakes his head. "Nope. Not a single day."

"What a charmed life," Gigi says.

"What are you guys talking about?" Arlo asks as she walks in from the back of the shop.

Gigi waves her bagel in our direction. "Being afraid and how these two bozos have never been afraid a day in their lives."

"Men have it easy," Arlo says, rolling her eyes. "They don't have a clue."

"We're not clueless," Stone tells her.

"Yeah. You are. Why are we talking about this?" Arlo asks, taking a seat at Carmello's station.

"Asher doesn't understand that Tate's attitude is

because she's scared and not because she's still acting like a shitty teenager."

Arlo clicks her tongue. "It's totally anger. I've been there. Helplessness is a horrible feeling. She's trying to fight someone because there's no one she can actually fight. It's all she can do."

"You've been there?" I ask, surprised by her admission.

"Yep. I was a foster kid. Most of my life was spent in fear. At least, the bits I can remember."

My stomach turns at her admission. I never put much thought into what she went through growing up in foster care. I barely know anything about her past, especially what she dealt with in her life.

"I'm sorry," I tell her.

Arlo waves off my sympathy. "I am who I am today because of what I went through. Would I change it if I could? Yeah. Would I change it if I knew my life wouldn't be what it is right now? Not a fucking chance. My life's too good now."

"That's so sweet," Gigi says to her. "I can't imagine life without you in the family."

"Is this a chick thing?" Stone asks.

I smile, ready to take cover if Arlo or Gigi starts throwing shit at us. "Which part?"

"The feelings and the fear."

I nod. "I think it is."

"Don't be assholes," Gigi warns us. "Give Tate a chance. Be cool."

"Tate's the shit. She's nothing like she used to be," Stone says, solidifying what Gigi said earlier.

"Yo," a voice calls from the front of the shop. "We need to talk."

"Fuck," Stone growls. "That's never good news."

"Nope." I climb to my feet, knowing Uncle Thomas is here to deliver news he didn't want to say over the phone.

"Here we go," Gigi says, peeling her ass off her seat and walking toward the front.

I brace myself for the bullshit he's about to spew. He never comes with anything good and never stops at the shop for no reason. He's too busy with work to do that, and chitchat isn't his strongest suit.

"Hey," Gigi says, rushing up to wrap her arms around him.

He doesn't hesitate as he hugs her back. "Hey, kid."

I stare at him, trying to decide what his body posture and expression are conveying, but I got nothing. He's good at masking, hiding things behind a tough, steely exterior. Uncle James has mastered the skill too, but Uncle Thomas is the king.

"What's wrong?" Stone asks at my side.

Uncle Thomas pulls out of Gigi's embrace. "I'm here about Tate."

The door to Lily's piercing room opens. "I'm here. I'm here," she says, rushing to the front of the shop to join us.

"Is this everyone?" Uncle Thomas glances around, waiting for more people to come out of the back.

"They're coming in later," Lily tells him as she comes to a screeching halt at my side. "What's up?"

Uncle Thomas crosses his muscular arms over his chest. His size and ability to retain his muscle mass are impressive for a man of his age. "I put feelers out to a few contacts across the state…"

"Like Morris?" Gigi asks.

Thomas nods. "It took a few days for them to get back to me after they gathered some intel."

Morris is a friend of the family of sorts. He used to be high up in an MC, but they're now defunct and not necessarily in good standing among the other MCs in the state, who are pissed.

Gigi and Tamara know him well, from years ago when they ran into some trouble. Then there's the fact that Morris plucked Pike from a bad situation and gave him a place to live. Mammoth knows him the best since he was a member of the MC and worked under Morris for years.

"What did they say?" I ask, but I know it's nothing good.

He wouldn't be here with good news.

He lets out a long, exaggerated sigh. "There are a few people down here searching for Tate. They're out for blood, but not before they'd like to have a *talk* with her."

My stomach turns at the way he says talk. "And by talk, you mean…" I let my voice die down, wanting him to fill in the blank.

"I don't even want to think about it," Uncle Thomas mutters. "I just wanted you to know they're here, and to keep your eyes open for anything out of the ordinary."

"Like what?" Lily asks, leaning against me with a small amount of her weight. I can feel the anxiety radiating off her.

"Anything. Someone following you in their car. Anyone staring at you a little longer than normal at the store. They could be anywhere and everywhere."

Fuck. It's like a nightmare. I hate the idea of looking over my shoulder at every moment, waiting for the boogeyman to snatch me.

"I'll inform Tate, but I wanted to let you guys know. We're trying to arrange a sit-down to straighten shit out and turn their eyes toward the real target," Thomas explains. "You see any shady shit, you call me or James immediately. Do not try to handle shit on your own. Got it?"

We nod in unison.

"Good. Good. I'm out. Angel's waiting for me at home to take her to dinner."

"Thanks for the update," I tell him.

He lifts a hand and marches out the door, disappearing into the setting sunshine like a morally gray superhero.

"Do you think Uncle Thomas ever killed anyone?" Lily asks softly.

All eyes in the room turn to her.

"What? No," Gigi says, but her voice holds no conviction.

"If anyone has, he has," Stone adds. "The man is scary as fuck."

A laugh bubbles out of Lily. "That's ridiculous. He's a sweet man."

I can't stop a loud bark from coming out of me. "He's not sweet."

"He is," Lily argues. "He always has been. He's like a big teddy bear."

"I don't ever want to know what he and James did in the past," Arlo says. "I've studied my father-in-law, and while the man is so darn sweet he makes my teeth hurt sometimes, I'm thankful every day I'm not on his bad side."

"Well, I'm thankful they and the guys at ALFA are on our side. The MC won't know what hit them," I say, lying through my damn teeth.

I said I'd never felt fear before, but in this moment, I feel a twinge creeping into my body, and I don't like it.

CHAPTER 23
OLIVE

"DO YOU MISS CHICAGO?"

"Of course. It's an amazing city."

"I've never been." I curl my feet underneath me as I hold a pillow against my front, tucked into the corner of the couch. "I heard it's great, though."

"You'll have to come visit."

Tate's been nothing but pleasant since Asher left. She's much tamer than she was the first time I met her at Inked. It's like she's growing more comfortable and feeling safer than she did before.

"I would love that. Maybe Asher will take me there."

"Come in the summer. Winters are brutal." Tate pulls her hair behind her head, wrapping her fingers around the base to make a ponytail. "It's the only time I think of moving."

"The summers are brutal here too. I don't know what's worse."

"Chicago," Tate snorts. "It's nowhere as beautiful there either. Have you seen dirty snow?"

I wrinkle my nose. "I have in pictures."

"Everything is either white or brown for months on end. I was in my car last winter, and it said the temperature was fifteen below zero. Not the wind chill…the temperature."

"I would literally die." I let my mind wander, trying to imagine what fifteen below would feel like. I've only ever lived in warm weather regions, and no matter how hard I try, I draw a blank.

"You ever have your fingers and face burn from cold? It's similar to being singed by a fire."

I shake my head. "I've burned myself on a hot pan, and then there's the sun here, but never by cold."

"Both suck ass."

"Yeah," I mutter. "I'm sure."

"Where were you before this? I heard Gigi say you just moved back."

"Texas."

Tate pretends to vomit. "That may be worse than here."

"It's hotter there, and the scenery is nowhere near as pretty as it is around here." I enjoyed living in Texas, but I'd never go back unless I absolutely had to.

There's a knock on the door, and my heart drops.

Tate bounds off the couch, rushing toward the front of the house. "Wings are here."

"Tate," I call out, unfolding my legs to stand. "Wait. You need to—"

But before I can say another word, she flings open the door. "Hey," she says to the person standing in the shadows of the front porch.

He takes a step to the right, coming into view in the light by the front door. "Gotcha," the man says, reaching out and grabbing Tate before she has a chance to react.

"Let me go!" she screeches as he pulls her inside.

He kicks the door closed with the bottom of his boot and yanks her arm hard, making her shriek in pain.

I rush toward them, but Tate screams, "No!"

I stop, my feet almost sticking to the wooden floor. "Don't hurt us," I plead.

The laugh that comes out of the man makes my hair stand on end. "Bitch, shut up and sit down before I knock you out."

The air inside my lungs evaporates as my heart stutters in my chest. I can't move. It's as if I'm paralyzed, something I've never experienced before in my entire life.

He reaches behind him, slipping his hand into his shirt, and pulls out a gun.

I gasp as my knees wobble.

"Sit down, or I'll use this sooner than I planned," he threatens.

I back up, reaching for anything to keep myself upright. My body is shaking so badly, it's a miracle I haven't fallen to the floor already.

"She's innocent," Tate tells the man who has the gun pointed in my direction. "Leave her alone. Your beef's with me, not her."

My hand catches the edge of the couch before my bottom. I need to do something. I want to do something. I stare at Tate and the straggly-haired man, praying he doesn't hurt her.

"You traitorous bitch," the man seethes.

"Logger, I'm not. I swear."

He yanks on her arm, causing her to go up on her tiptoes before he forces her to the floor. "You and I are going to have a little talk," he says, pointing the barrel of the gun toward her forehead. "I knew you were trouble from the minute I laid eyes on you, Tate. You have thirty seconds to start talking, or I'm going to start putting holes in you." He turns his face toward me, along with the gun. "Or her."

My bottom lip trembles as tears sting my eyes. This isn't how I wanted it all to end. I never thought I'd go out this way. I'm too young to die…too good. Who the hell am I kidding? I know there's no rhyme or reason to death, and eventually, it comes for us all in the end. There's no escaping it, no matter how hard we try.

"Why do you think it was me?" Tate says to the man.

He reaches back with his free hand and strikes her across the face. "Dumb bitch," he growls.

She folds over, grabbing at her cheek. "Fuck," she hisses. "It wasn't me, Logger."

"Talk," he snaps, pointing the gun back at her head.

I reach into my pocket, keeping my phone behind my back, and press on the screen. I don't know what the hell I'm hitting, but I'm hoping I'm calling someone…anyone. I miss the days of buttons instead of a flat-panel screen.

I drop the phone behind my back, leaving the line open for anyone on the other end to hear. The shop's only five minutes away. Tate doesn't need to keep the man talking for long, just long enough for Asher and the gang to get here and rescue us.

"I loved Rowdy. We've been friends and fuck buddies for years. But we ended a long time ago."

"And you were a jealous bitch who couldn't keep her goddamn mouth shut. You just had to pay him back for breaking your heart."

Tate glares up at Logger, her cheek a deep shade of pink where she was struck.

That's going to leave a nasty bruise.

Tate laughs softly, and it quickly bubbles over into a fit of hysterics. "That's the dumbest shit I've ever heard."

"What?" He leans forward, getting right in her face and personal space.

She keeps laughing, staring him straight in the eye. "I'm the one who ended the relationship, Logger. I'm the one who was done with the fun and games. Why the hell would I stop seeing Rowdy and then turn him in to the cops?"

Logger straightens, but his anger doesn't seem to fade. "Do women need a reason to do spiteful shit?"

"Does he have other enemies?" Tate asks him.

Logger squares his shoulders, steadying the gun. "We all do."

Tate rolls her eyes in defiance. "Exactly. Why the hell do you think it would be me?"

"You're the best suspect. You're not one of us. Never have been, and never will be."

"Do you have people out looking for any other suspects?"

"Only you."

"When I walked away from Rowdy, I walked away from the club…the life. I'm not built to be a side chick, Logger. I'm old lady material, but Rowdy wasn't willing to settle down."

"Babe, his name is Rowdy. What the fuck did you think?"

"I thought he'd eventually realize he didn't need anyone else. That I was enough for him."

Logger howls out a laugh but doesn't move the gun away from her. "Women always think their pussy is magical and it'll be the one that brings a man to his knees. A bunch of delusional bitches."

I've never been this close to a biker, only having seen the Hollywood version. The real-life one isn't as handsome or romantic as they're made out to be. The man has a gun in his hands, ready to murder two innocent women for no damn reason.

"Take me to Spades to talk."

"Spades doesn't want to see your mug, Tate. He's had enough of your shit to last a lifetime."

"Please," Tate begs the man with her hands folded together as she holds them up to him. "I need this to be over."

"No!" the man shouts. The quickness with which he can change emotions makes me dizzy. "This is your one chance to prove your innocence, and I'm your judge, jury, and executioner."

"Why the fuck should I talk to you when you already believe I'm guilty?"

I touch my chest, wanting to scream at Tate to shut the fuck up and stop throwing attitude at the bad guy with the weapon that can kill us both in the blink of an eye.

Logger bends over, bringing his head even with the gun. "Listen, little girl, I give no shits about pulling this trigger. You wouldn't be the first one to take their last breath at my hands."

"I didn't do it!" Tate screams in his face.

Logger lunges forward, snatching Tate by the hair,

making her neck bend in the most unnatural way. "You keep saying that, but you're not giving me a reason to believe you."

Tate's hands claw at Logger's hands, trying to get herself free. "I'm telling the goddamn truth."

"Give me another name."

Tate's eyes flash with anger as Logger releases her hair. "Why don't you try one of those whores at the clubhouse? They're always listening, trying to find a way to get their foot in the door and ass on the back of a bike."

The front door flies open, smashing into the wall behind it. I jump, falling to the floor and covering my head. It's irrational. It's not like my hands are somehow going to stop a flying bullet.

"Drop it," the deep voice says. "You're outnumbered."

I peer up through my fingers to go see who's come to our rescue. It's James and Thomas, Asher's uncles, their guns drawn and aimed in Logger's direction.

"You might as well shoot me," the guy tells them, keeping the gun trained on Tate. "I can't go back without handling the problem."

"She didn't do it," James bites out. "She's innocent. No one needs to die today."

I watch in horrific fascination as a real-life episode of *Sons of Anarchy* plays out in front of me. Never in a million years did I think I'd be put in this situation.

"Please, Logger," Tate begs. "It wasn't me. I'd

never betray the club or Rowdy. My grandfather's a freaking mafia guy. I was raised to keep my mouth shut."

Her grandfather was a mafia guy? I know about the history of Chicago and organized crime, but I never thought the Gallos were somehow entrenched in that world. Mind freaking blown.

James takes a step closer. "You kill her, and your club will never know a moment's peace. Do you want Santino and the boys as enemies? You kill his granddaughter, and there will be blowback…from both sides of the law. Not for you, though—you'll be just as dead as her—but for everyone else you care about."

"I talked to Spades," Thomas says, but he keeps his gun pointed at Logger. "He listened to what I had to say. He's calling you off and dropping the entire thing."

Logger scrunches his face. "What?" He shakes his head. "That's bullshit."

Thomas lifts his chin at Logger. "Call him."

With one hand still holding the gun, Logger reaches into his back pocket and fishes out his phone. He taps the screen with his thumb and then balances it on his shoulder. "Yo."

Logger's eyes don't move from us, and his body posture never changes. I wish he'd put the call on speaker. We're either about to be caught in a hail of bullets or nothing's going to happen at all. I'd like to be able to brace myself for the worst instead of leaning into the best and being wrong.

The intensity in Thomas's and James's gazes makes my heart sputter. There's a power that practically vibrates off them. They have a totally different aura than they had at their parents' house for the family dinner.

"Understood." Logger's gaze finally shifts, but he doesn't lower the gun. "Got it." Logger pulls the phone from his shoulder and jams it into the back pocket of his jeans that look like they were last washed when the Backstreet Boys were on the top of the music charts.

"Are you going to lower the gun or draw this out longer?" Thomas asks, standing still as a statue.

Logger blows out a long breath before finally letting his arms lower to his sides. "Fuck," he growls. "I'm sorry, Tate."

I'm sorry, Tate? Is he serious? Like saying those three little words makes up for holding a gun to her head and throwing her around the living room like she's a rag doll.

Tate crumples forward. "It's okay, Logger," she whispers into the area rug. "Just go."

James and Thomas lower their guns, but I have a feeling that if shit shifted, they could fire in an instant.

"I'm sorry, Tate," Logger repeats and hunches over, almost kneeling in front of her. "Nothing personal."

She peers up at him, her eyes swimming with tears. "Fuck off," she hisses, flattening her palms against the carpet, and digs her fingers into the fibers of the rug. "You, Spades, Rowdy…you can all fuck off."

Logger makes a slow nod. "Fair enough, kid." He rises to his feet, barely meeting the gazes of Thomas and James. "I'm out."

Thomas puts his arm out, stopping Logger when he tries to saunter out the front door. "If I ever see you around here again…"

"Noted," Logger mutters.

Logger and Thomas stare at each other for a moment before Thomas drops his arm, letting Logger pass.

When his boots sound on the front porch, I pull in a deep breath and crumple over as the life-threatening panic leaves my body.

CHAPTER 24
ASHER

"LET GO OF ME," I bark out, struggling against Pike's grip on my arms.

"Don't be a moron." He tightens his hands on my biceps. "You're going to go in there and get everyone killed, including Olive. Be fucking smart."

I stop fighting against his hold and narrow my eyes to catch a glimpse of Olive in the living room. "Where the fuck is she?"

"She's okay. If she weren't, they would've already shot that fucker."

I hate when he makes sense. I know what he's saying is true, but it doesn't make it any easier not to run into the house and carry out Olive, avoiding a spray of bullets.

As soon as I heard what was going on, I called Uncle James. Luckily enough, they were already on their way to my place to talk to Tate about some new information they'd received from Spades, the president of the MC, who was after Tate.

"There's movement," Nick says, lifting his chin toward the front of the house.

A man rushes from the door as Pike releases me. My legs move before I can even think, hauling ass to the porch. When I make it to the doorway, Thomas is near Tate, crouching over to pick her up off the floor, and James is on his way to Olive.

"I got her," I say, rushing in front of him.

Olive's eyes meet mine and instantly flood with tears. "Asher," she rasps out, her voice barely a whisper.

Olive's always been put together, but this experience, with a gun being pointed at her and Tate, has her rattled. Rightfully so, too.

"I got you," I whisper, holding her tightly against my chest and scooping her up off the floor. "You're safe."

"Oh my God, Asher," she sobs into my shirt, her fingertips twisting into the cotton. She's shaking and fighting against the rush of adrenaline now that it's over.

I brush my lips against her temple. "You're okay," I repeat, wanting the words to permeate her core. "No one will hurt you."

"Tate," she mumbles. "Tate."

I fall backward, landing on my ass, and settle Olive on my lap. "She's okay too. It's over," I say, brushing the hair away from her damp cheeks. "I'm sorry. I'm so, so sorry."

She shouldn't have been put in this situation. It's my fault. Entirely my fault. Olive could've died tonight, an innocent victim of Tate's fucked-up romantic life.

Olive tips her head back, peering up at me. "It's not your fault," she says like she's reading my mind. "I'm glad I was here with her. She was so…"

I squeeze my eyes shut, trying to wrestle with the images of a gun being held on the two of them. The terror on their faces as they did what they could to stay alive.

"She was so strong, Asher. Tate is amazing. She's fierce."

I gaze in Tate's direction, finding her standing with her arms wrapped around Thomas's waist. Other than a few tears, she looks strong and steady.

"You should be proud of her."

"I am," I tell Olive, stroking her back slowly and softly. "I'm proud of you too."

She held it together. As together as someone in her situation could, especially never having had her life in that type of danger.

Olive curls tighter against me and sags, resting her head on my shoulder with her face toward me.

"I'll never put you in that situation again."

"You can't promise that, and you didn't put me in this situation."

"But I did."

"Nope." She snaps her response. "I'm just glad I was able to get you on my phone."

"Thankfully, Thomas and James were already on their way here and beat me to the door."

She sucks in air between her teeth. "That would've been bad. It could've ended very differently."

"It would've." I hate to think about what could've happened. I would have run in half-cocked and angry, getting myself shot at the bare minimum. Whatever it would've taken to keep the girls safe.

"Thank you," Tate says to Uncle James, wrapping her arms around him. "I don't know how to thank the two of you."

"Don't mention it, kid. We're family. This is what we do. You're safe now," James says to her, squeezing her tightly before he kisses her hair.

"I don't know what you said to Spades, but thank you."

"I'm glad he finally listened. He's not a stupid man, and he didn't want the trouble following this wrong path would bring to him and his club. Rowdy had spoken to him too and vouched for you."

Tate untwists herself, peering up at my uncle, who towers over her. "He did?"

"Yeah. He made sure Spades understood you weren't to be touched and that you weren't the one who ratted him out."

"I wonder who talked?"

"That's between that person and the club. I don't care who they are as long as it wasn't you."

"I'd never talk, Uncle."

Thomas takes a step closer to James and Tate. "Talking to law enforcement about a crime isn't bad, Tate. We wouldn't have cared if you did. The problem stems from the club handing out punishment to anyone in our family. Don't ever feel like you can't tell anyone when shit goes bad. Got me?"

She nods. "I got you, but I don't think my gramps would feel the same."

"Fucking Santino," James mutters, glancing at the ceiling while he shakes his head. "The man has perpetually been on the wrong side of the law. Don't listen to him."

Tate smiles. "He likes the gray area."

"Gray?" Uncle Thomas laughs. "The man lives in the black. He wouldn't know the right thing to do if it hit him in the ass."

"He sounds interesting," Olive says, and her body stops shivering as if she's finally realized she's safe.

Tate crosses her arms with a shit-eating smirk on her face. "Then are we calling the cops now to tell them what happened?"

James's headshake is quick. "Nope. We're keeping this in-house."

Tate raises an eyebrow, staring at my uncle. "Living in the black too, Unc?"

"The gray, kid. I'm all gray," Thomas tells her.

Olive snorts. "They're funny."

"They're something," I mutter.

Olive's grip on my shirt loosens, and she starts to shift. "I'm okay now."

"Are you sure?" I ask, not wanting her to get up before she's ready. "You might still be in shock."

She shakes her head as she starts to push herself up. "I need to stand."

I understand the fake it till you make it mentality, but in this moment, I think she's pushing too much and too quick.

"But…"

Olive lifts her hand as she stands tall. "No buts, Asher. I'm fine. I promise."

Tate, James, and Thomas look in our direction, watching Olive.

"We good?" Uncle Thomas asks.

"We're good," Olive replies.

Uncle Thomas gazes in my direction, and I give him a slight nod, knowing he's looking for confirmation. There's no use in fighting it. Olive's as headstrong and stubborn as any woman in my family.

"You want us to take her for the night?" Thomas tips his head in Tate's direction.

Tate stares at me, giving me pleading, puppy-dog eyes.

"No," Olive answers before I have a chance to reply. "I want her to stay here."

I do my best to hide my annoyance. It's not that I don't love my cousin, but I'd like the night alone to talk to my girl about what just happened. She needs time to fully wrap her head around the fact that she almost just died.

"You sure?" Tate asks Olive.

Olive nods. "I have a bottle of vodka with our names on it."

Tate's smile is immediate and big. "You read my mind."

"Oh boy," I mutter.

Olive doesn't have a clue that Tate grew up in a bar and can probably hold her liquor better than most men more than twice her size.

"We're out," Uncle James announces as he smacks Thomas on the shoulder and pitches a thumb toward the door. "Let's ride."

No other words are spoken by my uncles before they disappear into the night, leaving like nothing happened.

Tate runs across the room and wraps her arms around Olive. "I was so scared for you."

Olive holds Tate tightly. "I was so scared for you."

A few days ago, they were strangers, but now they sound like best friends who went through some shit together that no one else would understand.

"You were so brave," Olive says as they sway together.

Tate pulls back to look at Olive. "Me?" Tate laughs softly. "You were brave."

"I hid behind the coffee table. I don't think that would earn me any awards for bravery."

"You stayed calm and quiet," Tate explains before they go back to hugging each other.

"You were amazing," Olive says. "You were fierce, girl. So damn fierce."

"It wasn't the first gun barrel I've stared down."

Olive's arms slip away from Tate. "What?"

Tate gives her a mischievous smirk. "Long story."

"Well then, it's a good thing that we have an entire bottle of vodka and more than a couple hours to kill."

"Hello," I call out, waving a hand. "I'm here."

Tate glances my way without a single fucking care in the world anymore. "Then we'll grab three shot glasses instead of two."

"Do you think drinking vodka is the best idea right now?" I ask.

They both turn their entire bodies to face me. Olive's hand is on her hip, and one eyebrow is raised. Tate crosses her arms, ready to throw her always-there attitude my way.

"Really?" Tate asks. "After all that…you want us to stay sober?"

"Asher," Olive says softly, shaking her head.

The last thing I want is two drunk, hysterical women, but I also don't want two sober, hysterical women either. I think after they've had more than a few minutes to decompress, the realization of what just happened is going to come crashing down on them.

"I think it's more of a tequila night," I respond, wanting to give them what they want, but at least with an alcohol that'll put them out sooner than later.

If they're passed out, they're not scared. If they're passed out, they're not mad. If they're passed out, they're not crying.

And tequila is the best thing to make that happen at a quicker pace. We could be here all night sipping vodka, and I'm not about to let that happen.

"You got lemon?" Tate asks, unfolding her arms from in front of her as she starts to drop the wall she keeps up around me the most.

"Of course. I'm not a monster," I tell her.

"Debatable," she mumbles before grabbing Olive's hand and pulling her toward the kitchen. "I'll get the lemon. You get the glasses."

I know I'm going to regret this in the morning. The only thing worse than two drunk women is three people with a massive hangover, two of them of the opposite sex.

The tequila goes down easy. A little too easy for Tate and Olive. They barely wince with each swallow. An hour later, they're swaying in their chairs, talking louder than normal—which, for Tate, is always loud—and giggling.

I'm still sober, pretending to slam back the drink,

but wanting to keep my wits about me. Right now, they're happy, but with all the alcohol in their systems, that could change in a split second, sending them into a crying fit.

Olive stands, waving her hand to get our attention. "Tate, the way you looked that asshole in the eyes and said 'shoot me' was fucking insane. You showed no fear. You're a goddess."

Tate gives a mock bow. "The man didn't have the balls big enough to shoot me. I called his bluff."

I run my hand down my face, muttering a slew of curse words under my breath that neither of them can hear since they're too busy laughing.

"You should've seen her, Ash," Olive says, slinging her arm around me before pressing her lips to my cheek. "She was amazing."

This must be the fifth time I've heard the replay of the events. Each time, it gets a little more dramatic, with a few embellishments thrown in.

"You too," Tate says, stalking over to the speaker to turn up the song. "I need to dance."

"Me too," Olive breathes out as she glides away from me to join Tate.

They dance around the living room, shaking their asses, and screaming the lyrics at the top of their lungs.

I watch them as they dance, and I'm relieved that what happened earlier didn't land someone in the hospital—or worse, the morgue.

Olive kept her wits about her, and Tate stared death in the eye, willing to sacrifice herself to keep Olive safe.

I'm exhausted, but I'll stay awake, waiting for them to get too drunk to move, think, or dwell on anything that happened.

How long can they possibly last with so much tequila in their system?

CHAPTER 25
OLIVE

THERE'S A POUNDING, and it feels like it's coming from deep inside my head. I grunt and roll over, careful not to fall when I feel the edge.

"Open up. I know you're in there," a man's voice says before the pounding starts again.

The voice sounds like my brother's, but he's hundreds of miles away and has no idea where I am.

"You can't ignore me forever," he says, hitting the door faster and harder than before.

I want to move and answer the door, but my body has other plans, and so does my mind. I still feel drunk, and the thought of opening my eyes to see sunlight has me wishing I could crawl into a dark hole and stay there for the next few days.

There are footsteps in the room. "I got it," Asher says. "Don't everybody move at once."

"It's your house," Tate tells him as I sling my arm over my face, hiding my eyes.

There's a creak followed by a "Hey" from Asher.

"Where is she?" the man asks.

"It's nice to see you again too, River," Asher says.

My eyes snap open underneath my arm. "Fuck," I groan, rolling to the side and falling off the edge of the couch. My knees hit the wood floor first, but I don't yelp even though I'll have a bruise there tomorrow.

"Ouch," Tate winces and then grabs her head. "Make the pain stop."

She's feeling it too. The aftereffects of the tequila from last night. She lurches forward, covering her mouth with her hand. Tate mutters something against her palm before taking off toward the bathroom.

"What. The. Hell?" River bites out.

I glance up as he pushes Asher to the side and rushes into the house. He's in front of me a second later, trying to help me off the floor.

"Don't," I snap, ripping my arm from his grip.

"What the hell happened to you?"

I stare down at the floor while I'm on all fours, and my stomach is threatening to do the same thing Tate's is. "I'm fine."

"You don't look fine."

I giggle at the stupidity of my brother. I've seen him drunk or hungover more times than I care to remember. "It was only a little tequila."

"A little?" he whispers, crouching over me. "That looks like more than a little."

I peer up, the sunlight in the room instantly making me see spots. "We were letting off a little steam."

River's pointed glare turns to Asher. "See what you've done to her? Olive's never been a drunk, and she's been here less than a week and she's already hungover."

Asher leans back against the front door, arms crossed in front of his chest, not looking like he gives an actual shit about what River's saying. "I didn't do that to her. That was entirely her and Tate."

River's eyes move toward the hallway where Tate went. "Who the fuck is Tate?"

I hear a loud retching sound as Tate empties part of the contents from last night's drinking party into the toilet.

"My cousin," Asher says.

"And my friend," I explain, hating the hypocritical judgment in my brother's eyes.

She'll always be that. There's no way you can go through a near-death experience with someone and not feel a natural, eternal bond.

"You're a mess," River says and again tries to help me up from the floor, but I push him away.

"Stop," I warn him, not willing to put up with any of his bullshit right now. "I'm fine. We're all fine."

River falls back, landing on his ass. "I knew he

would ruin you and I was right, but I didn't think it would happen this fast."

Somehow I find the strength to push myself backward, sitting the same way he is. I don't need a mirror to know I look like hell. I feel like it too. But that doesn't matter right now. Not with River in front of me. "You're going to judge me?" I touch my chest, closing one eye to block some of the mind-splitting pain I feel from the light filling the room.

"I'm judging him." River points his thumb behind him to Asher, who looks completely unfazed by the conversation.

Asher rolls his eyes and shakes his head. "Asshole," he whispers so low that neither of us can hear it, but luckily, I'm great at reading lips.

I glare at my brother. "He didn't make me drink, and the last time I checked, I was a full-grown adult. I'm allowed to have a few shots of tequila whenever I want to, and I don't need to ask for permission from you or him."

"It's my job to look after you."

I turn up my nose, trying to keep my anger in check. "It's not your job." I let out a sardonic laugh. "I've spent my entire life looking after you about most things, River. Your self-preservation instinct kicked in later than most people. No one's ever looked after me, including you. I'm the responsible one. The sensible one. Always have been, and always will be. But you…" I swallow the sandpaper laced with tequila that's coating the inside of my mouth. "You were allowed to be wild and free because you were a boy. Well, that shit stops today."

River sits in stunned silence, and I don't give him a chance to reply before I continue.

"I will do what I want, when I want, and it's none of your business. You're not my parent or protector, and stop acting like you can control my life. You can either be happy for me or show yourself out. Got it?"

River's eyebrows are almost at his hairline. "I got it, Oli," he whispers and glances down at the floor. "I thought I was looking out for you."

"Well, don't. I don't need it."

He lifts his hands. "Understood."

"How did you find me anyway?" I ask as Tate walks back into the room, wiping her mouth with a white washcloth.

"That sucked," she mutters before collapsing back onto the couch I just vacated.

"I called Tamara," River replies, ignoring Tate's groaning as she tries to get comfortable. "She told me you were here."

I figured as much. She's the only person in Asher's family River had a relationship with that hadn't completely soured before we moved.

"What did she say?" I press, wondering if she knows about what happened last night and filled in River. It's the only reason he could be acting like a complete and utter shithead about Asher. There's no love lost between them, but he's being a little over the top about our relationship…more than his usual.

"She said there was an issue with your apartment."

I rest my head against my hand as I prop my elbow on my knee. The pounding inside my skull hasn't stopped, and right now, it feels like it never will. Tequila and I don't mix. Never have, and it's clear we never will.

"A person in the leasing office stole the check and never put in my application for an apartment," I admit, hating to tell him I've been swindled.

River's eyes grow big. "What? Are you serious?"

I nod. "Yep. I showed up with all my things to get the keys, and they had nothing for me. No record of my visit, let alone a paper trail of the check or the paperwork I filled out."

"That's fucked up."

I nod my head slowly, gritting my teeth. "At least Asher opened his home to me, or else I don't know where I'd be right now."

Tamara either doesn't know what happened last night, or she knew enough not to fill my brother in on the fact that I could've easily died at the hands of an unhinged biker. Either way, I'm thankful River's in the dark.

"I can lend you the money to get your own place," he says, which sounds nice, but he's only saying that to get me away from Asher.

"No. I'm happy where I am." I glance at Asher, who's still watching silently from across the room. "I'm comfortable here, and I feel safe."

Tate lets out a grunt from her spot on the couch.

"This is far from campus," River adds, not seeming to think anything of Tate's noise. "It's not really optimal or practical."

"I need coffee," I mutter. I don't have the mental energy to argue with River.

"I'll make a pot," Asher says as he starts to move toward the kitchen.

"Make two," Tate calls out, raising her arm high in the air, but Asher doesn't respond as he walks out of the room.

"Stop being a douchebag," I tell my brother, lowering my voice so Asher can't hear. "I don't care what happened between the two of you when you were dumb teenagers over a girl you probably can't even remember the name of, but get the hell over it. Stop being an asshole and trying to ruin what I have going here."

River leans forward and says, "I remember her name, and so the fuck does he, Oli. It's cute that you want to play house, but in a week, you're going to be calling me about your broken heart and how Asher Gallo cheated on you."

"You are a douchebag," Tate whispers loud enough for River to hear. "Asher's one of the best."

River turns his icy glare toward her almost-lifeless body. "That's what all the women say."

"She's his cousin, Riv. I know you think of Asher as the same guy he was back then, but my question for you is…are you still that same guy too?"

River leans back and actually takes a moment to think about my question. "Well, no," he blows out as his shoulders relax. "I'm nothing like him."

"Neither is he."

"You don't know—"

"I do," I tell him in a stronger voice. "I do know, and if something happens and he breaks my heart, that's on me. That's my choice. My risk to take. You're my brother, and you're supposed to be there to support me, no matter what, just like I've supported you in all your decisions, either good or bad. And trust me, Riv…you've got a whole lot of bad ones sprinkled in there."

River shrugs. "I'm not the smartest one of us."

"Clearly," I grumble.

He blows out a long, steady breath. "I don't like it."

"You don't need to. He's not your boyfriend, but you can at least respect that I know what I'm doing and, when you're around him, treat him with kindness."

"That's asking a bit much, Oli."

I glare at him, and he throws up his hands.

"Fine," he snaps. "I'll do my best to be nice, but I can't promise it'll be easy."

"He doesn't need to be a major part of your life because he's a major part of mine."

"I thought we'd always be close."

I pull my legs against my chest, hugging my knees. "Our closeness will be entirely up to you. It'll depend on whether you can let go of the past and move on toward the future."

"Don't be a dick," Tate mutters as she throws her arm over her face. "Life's too short."

"You're happy?" River asks.

I nod. "Very."

"Okay. I'll make nice."

"River, you want a cup?" Asher asks when he walks back into the room with two mugs. He hands one to me before setting the other one on the coffee table next to Tate.

"Sure," River says, pushing himself up from the floor. "I can grab it."

Asher waves him off. "You're my guest. I'll get it."

"Can we talk?" River asks before Asher has a chance to disappear again.

"Sure," Asher replies, but I know that tone. He doesn't really want to talk to my brother, and I can't blame him. River can be a complete asshole—that much hasn't changed since he was a dumb teenager.

River follows Asher into the kitchen, not bothering to look back at me.

"That'll go well," Tate whispers before she flings her arm away from herself. She winces as the sunshine lands on her face. "Is this what a vampire feels like?"

I chuckle as I tighten my grip around the warm mug. "I'd assume it's worse for them."

Tate shifts to her side, squinting. "How can it be worse?"

"I think it's the whole bursting into flames thing that could be worse than a hangover," I tell her before taking my first sip, wishing it had the ability to wipe away the pounding inside my skull.

Tate feels around the coffee table until her hand finds the mug. "I'd take some flames if it meant the headache would go away." She brings the coffee cup to her lips and slurps the hot liquid before moaning.

I set my cup down next to the area rug and climb to my feet very slowly.

"Where are you going?" she asks me with one eye open, looking like she had the roughest night ever… which, technically, she did.

"To listen," I whisper.

Tate places her coffee back on the table and collapses back with a grunt. "Shitshow," she mutters, and she isn't wrong.

But there's no way I'm going to let them hash shit out without listening in.

River and Asher will bury the hatchet before he

leaves town, or there's going to be hell to pay later. The past is the past and needs to be left there.

We're building a future, and I want it to include my brother—as long as he can move beyond the sins of his and Asher's past.

CHAPTER 26
ASHER

"HEY."

I grind my teeth together as I grab another mug from the cabinet.

River Thornberry always thought he was better than everybody. How someone like him could have a sister as sweet as Olive is beyond me.

"Hey," I grit out. "You want cream and sugar?"

"Black."

I keep my back to him, muttering under my breath, knowing this isn't going to go as nicely as Olive hopes.

"So," he says as I pour his coffee, "you and Olive."

I can guarantee she sent him in here to make nice with me, but so far, he's striking out. He hasn't said much, and the statement he just made is laced with judgment and disapproval.

I turn around, holding the mug out to him instead of throwing it on him like I let myself fantasize about. "Yeah."

He doesn't hesitate in taking the coffee from me, but he doesn't take a sip. "You sure about it?"

I lean back, crossing my arms, and stare at him. "Never surer about anything in my life."

I don't expect River to understand, but this was always meant to be. We were thrown into each other's path for a reason, and I'm not going to ignore the universe's grand plan.

"I don't like it."

"You made that clear, River."

He was never someone to hide how he felt. I envied him for that when we were younger, but looking back on it, he was just an asshole. There's a fine line between being honest and being a dick. River could've been honest without doing his best to hurt people's feelings, which he did a lot back then.

"My sister deserves the best."

"I agree," I tell him, keeping my glare pinned on him.

"I don't want her to settle for less than she deserves."

"She's not."

He slides into a chair at my kitchen table, keeping his front facing me. "She's always had a soft spot for you, Asher. I worry she's not using her brain, but following her heart instead."

"Does your sister not use her brain often?"

I don't need to ask him that question. I already know the answer. Olive was never the type to do anything without putting a lot of thought into it. I'm sure that hasn't changed over the years, no matter what River says.

"No. Carefree isn't in her nature."

"Then why would she be different with me?"

He relaxes back into the chair, spreading his legs out. "She wouldn't," he says softly, unable to meet my eyes.

"I love your sister."

River's gaze snaps to my face. "Isn't it a little early to say that?"

I shake my head. "I've known your sister most of my life, River."

"But you haven't known her for almost a decade."

"Doesn't matter. The moment I laid eyes on her, I knew."

"You knew?"

"I knew she was the one for me."

"Unbelievable," he mutters under his breath.

"I'm not the same dumb kid who slept with your girlfriend in high school. He's been gone for a while. I'm sorry about what happened and how it went down. If I could go back and change things, I would in a fucking heartbeat if it meant that you wouldn't try to stop your sister and me from being together now."

"I don't want my sister to be with a cheater."

"Samantha was the cheater, River. Not me."

"You didn't have any respect for our relationship, Asher."

"Neither did Samantha." I remind him. I wasn't the only one who was wrong that day, but I took all the blame. "It's hard to say no to a girl who wants to suck you off when you're a horny teenage boy."

River winces, the wound still slightly raw. "I liked her."

"She didn't deserve your attention. Anyone who would do that when they're with someone else doesn't deserve shit."

River nods. "I know, but it didn't make it easier to take."

"You're still pissed about it, and the shit was ten fucking years ago. Were you going to marry her someday?"

He lets out a small laugh. "Fuck no."

"Then who cares? Why still be pissed at me about some insignificant chick?"

He shrugs and moves his hand back to his mug. "I don't know. I was so damn jealous of you."

"Of me?"

"Yeah, man. You had everything."

"You had the world by the balls too, River. It was a pretty fucking great time for both of us."

He pulls the mug to his chest and stares down into the dark liquid. "Not like you, though."

"Bullshit," I cough.

He brings his gaze to mine. "You had all the girls after you."

"You did too."

"You had this crazy big family that always had your back. You guys were all thick as thieves."

"Still are," I mumble.

"I hated you more for that than Samantha Maroni."

I raise my eyebrows, surprised by his admission. "Why, man? They were your friends too."

They were—at least until he lost his shit over Samantha. Then he became not only my enemy, but one to all my cousins and friends.

"Friends come and go, Asher. You could do no wrong in their eyes. They're family."

I snort. "I don't do much right either. They're a judgmental bunch that'll put me in my place faster than anyone else."

"Never felt that way."

"They'd kill to protect me, but that doesn't mean they won't rip me a new asshole when I fucking deserve it. And they're the same with Olive. They've taken her in and made her one of our own. They'd lay down their lives for her or eviscerate anyone who has a shitty thing to say to her."

"You had a built-in ride-or-die group."

"Yeah, I did and I still do, but that doesn't mean you can't get a piece of it too."

"They hate me," he mutters.

"Did Tamara say that when you talked to her?"

He shakes his head. "Nah, she was nice."

I bark out a laugh. No one describes my sister as nice except her children, but that's only because they're too small to understand the fierceness of their mother. "My sister is not nice."

"No," he says quickly. "She was nicer than I remember her being."

"We all mellow with time," I lie, knowing my sister hasn't calmed down a damn bit, and I worry she never will.

"There isn't a person in this family who wouldn't welcome you to the group with open arms. If things work out and your sister decides to stay with me, she'll officially become a member of our family, and by extension, that would make you one of us too."

"Hardly," he says, sounding defeated.

"I'm not lying. You want in, you're in."

"It's not that easy."

"Then you don't know my family."

I swear they'd welcome anyone to become one of us, always saying there's room for more. My grandma thinks everyone in the world deserves people, and there're no better people than ours.

"I could marry your sister and make it official."

"I don't think her husband would like that."

He frowns against his mug. "Naturally, she's taken. She was always the prettiest girl I ever knew."

"Maybe the mouthiest."

"Is she happy?"

I nod. "Mammoth makes her very happy."

"Mammoth," he grunts, "Of course her husband is a mammoth."

"He's a solid guy. I didn't like him much at first, but he's grown on me."

"You didn't like him?"

"Nah, he was a cocky bastard, but then I realized he's the only one who can handle Tamara. She'd run right over anyone less than him."

River laughs. "She was always a tough one. It's why I liked her."

I'm glad she was tough and that she didn't fall for River. I can't imagine having anyone other than Mammoth as a brother-in-law. He's one of the good ones, even though they had a rocky start.

"Can we at least get along for your sister's sake?" I ask, not wanting anything or anyone to come between us.

River stares up at me, studying my face. "You promise you'll treat her right?"

"She's my queen," I explain. "I will always put her first and protect her with my life, if need be. My cousins love her, my grandparents on both sides adore her. She's in good hands here, and she's not alone."

"She always craved being part of something bigger."

"She's got that now."

River smiles genuinely. "I'm good with it, but I'll have no problem breaking your legs if you do her wrong."

"I'm pretty sure you'd have to beat my family to the punch if that happens."

River chuckles as he sets the mug on the kitchen table. "It's going to take a lot for me to knock off that chip that's weighed heavy on my shoulders for years, Asher. But for the sake of my sister, I'll work on it. Just keep her happy, and it'll fall away eventually." He gets up and holds out his hand to me. "I want whatever is going to make her happy."

I take his hand and shake it firmly, but not aggressively. "Me too, River. I'd like it if we could be friends someday."

"Is it safe?" Olive asks, walking into the kitchen and looking around in the most dramatic fashion. "Do I need to call the cops?"

"Fuck the police!" Tate yells from the living room.

Olive giggles and then grabs her head. "Tate is a trip."

"What's her deal?" River asks, ticking his head toward the living room.

"She's a problem child."

"I'm grown!" Tate yells, listening to the conversation with her superhuman hearing.

"She's gotten into some trouble. She doesn't really mean fuck the police," I try to explain, because I don't want to get into the history of her grandfather with organized crime.

"I do!" she yells. "Fuck. My head."

"Why did you two get so drunk?" River asks Olive.

"We were just blowing off some steam," she says as she walks up next to me, leaning the side of her head against my bare arm. "It was a hectic day yesterday."

I almost bark out a laugh but somehow keep it inside. Hectic? That's not the word I'd use for it, but she's keeping that information from her brother. I don't fault her for it either. His head would probably pop off his shoulders and explode.

"We should meet up for dinner tomorrow. How long are you staying in town?" Olive asks her brother as I slide my arm around her and hold her waist.

"Just a few days."

"Where are you staying?" she prods.

"In Clearwater, on the beach. I rented a condo for a few days. I missed the ocean."

"Me too," Olive breathes. "The salt air, the sound of the waves."

River ticks his chin toward the view in the back. "This is impressive. I could live here without a second thought."

"Why don't you come back?" she asks him. "It would be nice to live close to each other again. We've been apart long enough."

"Maybe," he says, running his hand back and forth through his hair. "We'll see. You're going to stay after you finish school?"

She nods. "I plan to stay forever," she says, staring up at me. "I have too much here to stay for now."

"Fuckin' right," Tate chimes in. "Olive's one of us. Trauma sisters forever."

River's gaze moves toward the living room. "Trauma sisters?"

"Don't mind her. She's being silly." Olive smiles at her brother. "And she's still a little drunk."

"So, dinner…" River says, thankfully moving past Tate's outbursts. "Tomorrow?"

"Asher has to work," Olive says, giving me a sad smile.

"It's okay, love. You go. Enjoy an evening with your brother."

"When are you off again this week?" River asks.

"I'm booked solid through Saturday."

"Damn," he mutters. "That's too bad." But when he says that, there's no conviction in his voice.

"We have forever," I tell him, earning a squeeze from Olive.

CHAPTER 27
OLIVE

THREE MONTHS *later*

"Come here," Asher's Grandma Washington says to me as I place the last clean dish in the cabinet. "I want to talk to you, sweet girl."

In the last three months, she's become one of my favorite people. She's sassy and so full of life. So is his other grandmother, but there's something about Grandma Washington that draws me to her.

She pats the cushion of the chair next to her. "We haven't had a moment alone all day."

"I know," I say as I place the dish towel on the counter before sliding into the chair at her side. "I'm sorry."

She smiles at me in that way only a grandmother can. "It's okay, dear. There was a house full today."

The entire family showed up, but Brenda sucked the air out of the room like she always does. She gave a mini concert, featuring her favorite singer…Prince or the Artist Formerly Known as Prince, as he was known before his untimely death. I didn't know much about him before I met Brenda, but now I feel like I could write an entire biography without a problem.

She pushes a candy bowl in front of me. "Have some."

I take a piece of hard candy with a strawberry-like wrapper. "I like these."

"They were always my favorite." She places her hand over mine. "How are things with my grandson? Is he treating you right?"

"He's great."

"I don't have a problem hitting him with my shoe if he's misbehaving."

I shake my head and giggle, picturing her chasing after him with her old slipper in her hand. "He's the sweetest."

"Asher's the sweetest?"

"He is. I've never had someone so concerned with my happiness."

Her smile almost reaches her eyes. "His mama taught him right."

"Anthony treats Max like that too. I think he watched his daddy a lot growing up."

I've studied Asher's parents a lot over the last three months, and their relationship is everything I thought love should be.

"I wasn't sure about Anthony when I met him, but

that man has been full of surprises. I'm not sure anyone else could've ever dealt with my baby like he has over the years. He has the patience of a saint because Maxine is a handful. Always has been, and always will be."

"Really?" I ask, wondering what she was like when she was younger.

"Spitfire from the second she came out of me. She was a fussy little thing, and the moment she learned to walk and talk, she never stopped." Grandma shakes her head, smiling big. "Cutest little thing you ever did see."

"Was Asher more like his mom or dad when he was little?"

"He's definitely like his momma, but he has a heavy dose of his daddy too." She reaches into the bowl of candy and fishes out a partially unwrapped one. "Now, how's school going?"

"Really well. I've been working in the research center as part of my grad work."

She tosses the candy in the air, making it into the trash can in an impressive maneuver for someone of her age. "Do you know about my husband?"

I nod. "I do."

"It's a terrible condition. I watched him wither away. He was always so strong—" she shakes her head, and I can see tears filling her eyes "—but it took everything from him."

"I'm so sorry," I whisper and take her hand in mine.

"It's not your fault. It's no one's, but I'm thankful every day that there are brilliant people working on a cure so no one else has to suffer the way he did."

"I'll do my best."

Her fingers curl against mine. "It's all I can ask for, Olive."

Now it's my turn for my eyes to fill with tears. She's called me Kalamata since the day I met her, but just now, for the first time ever, she's used my real name.

"Baby," Asher says, and I turn my head, finding him staring at us with a look of confusion. "Ready to go?"

"Give me a minute."

He nods. "Just a few. I'm tired."

"Come kiss your granny," Mrs. Washington says to him and taps her cheek. "Right here."

Asher doesn't grumble as he strides across the kitchen and leans over, kissing his grandmother right where she touched.

"I love you, baby."

"Love you too, Gram," he whispers against her cheek.

"You two kids get out of here. I said what I needed to say. I'll have Brenda finish helping me."

"You sure?" I ask his grandmother, feeling bad that she'll have to listen to Prince the entire time.

"She's harmless. A little nutty, but harmless."

I giggle. "She's sweet."

Mrs. Washington's eyebrows rise as she tilts her head, debating what she wants to say. "That she is, dear," she says, deciding to be nice. "Now, go. Enjoy the rest of your evening alone together."

I lean over, giving her a kiss. "Thanks, Gram," I say, the words coming out naturally. She's been more of a grandmother to me than my own has been since the day I was born.

I've been in the Tampa area for three months now, and I've only seen my biological grandparents once during that time. I'd visit them every week if they allowed it, but they've made it clear they like their privacy.

Asher takes my hand and helps me up from my chair. "I grabbed some cake to take home," he tells me.

"I hope you grabbed two because I'm not sharing your grandma's German chocolate cake."

His grandma howls with laughter. "That's my girl."

"You're supposed to be on my side, Grammy."

She waves off Asher. "We girls got to stick together, baby."

Asher rolls his eyes. "Of course you do," he mutters.

Tamara pops into the kitchen with Riley curled

around her body. "We're going to the beach to watch the sunset. Do you guys want to come?"

Asher looks at me, waiting for my answer. "That sounds nice, but it's up to you," I say to him.

"Yeah, we'll go." He winks at me. "It's been a few weeks since we watched the sunset."

The last time we went, we spent more time making out than watching the sun disappear behind the horizon.

"We'll meet you there," Tamara says as she walks back out of the kitchen, and we follow her. "We have to stop home and grab a few things."

"Which beach?" Asher asks.

"Honeymoon Island."

"You good with that?" he asks me.

"It's perfect."

It's one of my favorite local beaches and the perfect spot to watch the sunset over the Gulf of Mexico.

Mammoth's waiting on the front porch with Jackson, trying to keep him under control as the kid blows off some extra energy generated by eating all the desserts at his great-grandma's. Mammoth looks completely unfazed, but he often looks like that.

"This kid needs to run around on the beach for a while tonight if we ever want to get him to sleep," Mammoth tells Tamara.

"That's the plan, big guy," she says, touching his shoulder. "We have to stop home first, though."

“Whatever you want, princess.”

“We’ll meet you two there,” Tamara says, walking off the porch with her husband. “See you in a bit.”

“Bye, Unkie Ash!” Riley yells as she’s carried away by her mother.

“You’ll see him in a bit, baby,” Tamara tells her daughter.

“Yay!” Riley cheers, raising her little fist in the air.

“She’s too much. She loves her uncle,” I say, standing with Asher on the front porch as we watch Tamara and Mammoth load the kids into the car.

“She’s my girl,” he says to me and brushes his lips against my cheek, “and you, too, of course.”

“I don’t mind sharing with her, but only her.” I smile as he lets out a deep grunt.

“See you in an hour.” Tamara gives me a little chin lift before folding her body into the car.

“I want to make a few stops on the way,” Asher says as he pulls me by the hand down the front steps. “We should get a bottle of champagne.”

“Fancy,” I tease. “What’s the occasion?”

“We survived a day with my family. That’s reason enough to drink, and you’re too sophisticated for beer.”

I snort, remembering more than a few occasions where I threw beer back like it was water. But I haven’t had a drop to drink since Tate. I can still taste the tequila on the back of my tongue anytime I think about that night.

"I'm not too good for beer. I like a cold beer on a hot summer night."

"Well, it's fall," he says, like somehow that would make sense. "Tonight's about champagne."

"Whatever you say."

I don't bother arguing. There's no point. Asher has a weird way of thinking about things, and no matter how many times we go round and round, he always digs in his heels harder and deeper. He can be so unmovable sometimes. He reminds me of River when he's like that. They both think funny, but maybe that has more to do with men in general than just the two of them.

An hour and two stops later, because the first one didn't have the right champagne, and we are in the parking lot of Honeymoon Island beach.

"It's so pretty here," I say, looking out the windshield beyond the parking lot to the ocean.

It's a hidden gem in the area. Tourists rarely come this far north of Clearwater, preferring to stay closer to their hotels and the easy-access beach within walking distance. Honeymoon Island is known to locals as one of the best places in the country to watch the sunset and cozy up with someone special.

"We have about an hour before sunset. Tamara texted and said they're on their way here."

"Did you bring a blanket?" I ask as I reach for the handle to the car door.

"I brought everything we need."

"You planned to come here tonight?"

He walks to the back of his SUV and pulls open the back. "I thought it would be a nice way to unwind after a day with the Washingtons." He grabs a blanket, the two bottles of champagne, and a mini cooler.

"What's in there?"

"Juice boxes for the kids."

"That's why you're their favorite uncle."

"I'm their only uncle."

I laugh and shake my head. "You're ridiculous. They have a ton of great uncles."

"I'm the only real one, though."

I take the blanket from his arms, trying to make it easier for him to carry the drinks for the six of us. I resist the urge to kick off my sandals and feel the warm sand between my toes until we make it to our final spot.

We find a place close enough to the water's edge where no one will sit in front of us and block our view. Asher and I are careful how we place the blanket, trying not to get any sand on top. It's useless, though. As soon as the kids start running around, they'll track half the beach onto the blanket before the last ray of sunshine is left in the sky.

"You want to look for shells?" Asher's eyes scan the beach in front of us. "There may be some left behind because it was high tide this afternoon."

"Sure," I tell him, loving to collect them to put in

jars. They're a pretty and cheap way to decorate my office in the house.

Asher takes my hand, but I pull back to kick off my shoes. I went too many years without feeling the soft powder between my toes.

"I don't know why you like it so much."

I smile up at him and shrug. "I'm weird."

He laughs. "You are, Oli. It's the worst feeling in the world."

"Stubbing your pinkie toe against the leg of a coffee table is the worst feeling in the world, not sand."

He winces, knowing exactly what I'm talking about.

"It's a perfect night." The warm breeze caresses my bare shoulders as I bend over and pluck a cracked shell from the sand. "Warmer than usual for this time of year." I inspect the shell, turning it over in my hand, admiring the soft pink coating the exterior.

"It is a perfect night," Asher says, kneeling down near me.

I turn toward him, finding him on one knee and holding out his hand. "Olive," he says softly and raises his arm. "I know this may seem early…"

The sparkle off his fingertips catches my eye. My heart stutters, stopping and starting again as the realization of what's happening settles in.

He's proposing.

Asher Gallo is going to ask me to be his wife.

The boy I crushed on and thought I'd never get to be with is going to ask me to spend the rest of my life with him.

"But I've never been happier than I have been the last three months. I truly believe we found each other again for a reason, and I want to make sure we never spend another moment apart. I love you, Olive Thornberry. I want you to be mine for eternity. Will you do me the honor of becoming my wife?" He holds up the ring like he isn't sure I saw it before.

My vision blurs, and tears stream down my face. "Yes, Asher. Yes!"

He grabs my hands because I'm too big of a mess to thrust my arm forward. The ring slides on easily, but the weight of it proves undeniably that it's there.

We're going to get married.

No longer will I be alone or at least feel that way. I'm gaining a husband and his entire big, crazy family.

Asher stands, sliding his muscular arms around me. "My wife," he whispers as he smiles down at me.

"My husband," I whisper back, flattening my front to his.

He bends his neck, taking my lips with his. I breathe him in, memorizing the moment.

The joy.

The excitement.

The endless possibilities.

CHAPTER 28
OLIVE

ONE YEAR LATER...

"I can't believe it's been a year since Asher proposed," Tamara says while she stands behind me, fixing my hair as she glances at me in the mirror.

"I know." I don't know where time went. It feels like yesterday when we ran into each other at the grocery store. A lot has happened in that time too.

I moved halfway across the country, moved in with Asher, and started at a new school. The days have flown by, melting into each other. I've never been so happy or felt so complete.

"Tomorrow's the day. Are you ready?" she asks, smoothing my hair down on top of my head into a seamless ponytail.

"I've never been more ready for anything in my life."

Life has changed for the better. Not just because

of school, but because of Asher and his entire family. I've never felt like I was part of something bigger until I moved back here. The Gallos took me in, making me feel like I'd always been there and was always meant to be there too.

"I called the restaurant," Gigi says, walking into the bedroom with her phone in one hand. "Everything's set. After the rehearsal on the beach, we'll be ready to rock 'n' roll."

"Thank you," I tell her, smiling at her reflection in the mirror.

"Damn, girl," Gigi says, followed by a whistle. "You're looking like a snack."

I snort. "Hardly."

Gigi shakes her head. "No, for real. Asher's going to lose his stinking mind when he sees you."

I glance down, staring at my dress. It's a little more revealing than I used to wear. But being with Asher has given me confidence I never thought I'd have. I've never felt more beautiful than I do when I'm with him, and his daily affirmations have done wonders on my self-confidence.

"I bet they don't make it halfway through the dinner before he wants to go home," Tamara says with a chuckle.

"Men are so easy," Gigi says, smiling at me. "I know you've learned that about our cousin."

"It's not too difficult to get him sidetracked sometimes."

"Ladies," a man's voice calls, knocking on the door.

The laughter in the room dies down immediately. I love my parents, but they know how to kill a good time. They're like throwing a bucket of ice water over a flame with their low energy about everything, including their kids.

I turn my gaze toward the hallway, finding my father standing there in his best suit.

"May we have a few moments with our daughter?" My mom moves to his side, curling her arm with his. "We won't be long."

Tamara's eyes meet mine. "We won't be far."

"It's okay," I say to her with a smile. "We'll be fine."

It's not like my parents are going to be mean. That requires an emotion, and that's never been their strong suit.

I turn on my stool at the makeshift vanity we set up in my office. "You came," I breathe out, surprised they made the trip a day early, even for their only daughter's wedding. "I thought you weren't getting in until tomorrow morning."

I don't dare stand. The heels Max chose for me are entirely too high for me. The less time I spend upright in them, the better. If I don't fall flat on my face walking on the sand later…it will be a miracle.

My mother enters the room first as soon as the girls are gone. "I wanted to make the rehearsal dinner and meet Asher's family." She's dressed in a casual sundress, never wanting to be too fancy. "And I hate traveling at night."

That is probably more the truth. My parents haven't bothered to meet his family in the year plus since we started dating, or even after we became engaged. They don't bother with anyone, even their own kids' future families. And my mother hates the dark and does her best to not be on the road after the sun sets.

"You look pretty, honey," my dad says as he stalks into the room. "The house is nice."

Dad had never lingered long on sentimental stuff, even when it comes to me. Many girls are Daddy's girls, but not me. And my father never wanted that kind of attention either. How he went from me looking pretty to the house in a split second only reinforces that point.

"Do you need anything?" Mom asks as her eyes move around my office, taking in all the books and pictures. "Anything at all?"

"No," I say because there's honestly no point. They're just being kind because they feel they should at least ask, but they don't really want to be put out. "We have it all under control."

My mother gives me a tight smile. "Well, that's great."

Dad shoves his hands into the front pockets of his

slacks. "We don't want to keep you. We know you're busy, but we'll catch up at the dinner."

What type of parents would think they're bothering their daughter by talking to her on the night before her wedding? My parents, of course.

I knew they were different. It was hard to ignore that fact when I knew what other kids' parents around me were like. But nothing truly drove the point home until I spent time with Asher's family. I knew then how much I really missed out on as a kid, and hell, even as an adult.

"Sounds good." I place my hands in my lap, clasping them together. They're not huggers. They're not Gallos. "We'll talk later." I give my mother back her same tight, non-emotional smile.

"Good," she replies with a slow nod before she spins on her heel and stalks out of the office with my father right behind her.

Tamara's back in the room first. "That was…"

"Weird?" I raise an eyebrow.

She nods. "I guess that's the right word."

My shoulders slump forward as a little bit of excitement slides out of me. "That's them. They're always weird. Distant. Cold."

Tamara wraps her arms around me, careful not to mess up my hair. "But you have us now," she whispers.

I can't stop a smile from spreading across my face. "Thank goodness for small miracles."

I can't imagine what my life would've been like if I hadn't run into Asher. I'd be alone, devoid of emotion. Would I follow in my parents' footsteps, not caring about anyone other than myself? Maybe, but I hate to think that would've been my fate.

"Look at you," Max, Asher's mom, says from the hallway, peeking her head inside the room. "You're simply stunning. I knew that dress would look fabulous on your frame."

Max's styling is spot-on. It's what she does professionally, and she begged me to let her help me pick out my dresses for the weekend's festivities. I couldn't say no. My biological mother may not care, but my soon-to-be mother-in-law is eager to smother me with love and acceptance. I'm not going to deny her or myself of it either. I lap it up, crave her kind of love, and am thankful every day that she came as part of the package with Asher.

"You were right," I tell her, climbing to my feet, careful to balance on the heels. "But these shoes."

Max chews on her lip as she watches me sway. "Lose them and go barefoot on the sand. I'll pack a pair of sandals for you for the restaurant afterward. I don't care how pretty something is, shoes especially, if they're going to be trouble or cause pain. Gimme." She motions with her hand for me to take them off and give them to her.

I collapse back onto the stool, prying the pretty

stilettos from my feet. "They're torture, but they are beautiful."

Max smiles as she takes them from me. "We'll save them for a shelf somewhere to remember the day. Some things are meant to be looked at, and others worn. This is not a wearing thing for you, honey."

My gaze drops to her footwear, which isn't very dissimilar from the pair she'd picked for me. "You do it so well, though, and I don't know how."

Max laughs. "Years of punishing my feet make it possible. You don't want to see them either. All the high heels make my feet look more like a pair on an alien than a person. My toes are all crooked and shit."

"That ain't no lie," Anthony says, walking up behind his wife and wrapping his arms around her middle. He rests his chin on her shoulder, hugging her. "But I love those damn things anyway."

"You better," she grumbles, melting into his embrace.

"You look beautiful, Olive. We're excited this day is here, and although you're already a member of this family, we couldn't be happier to finally make it official. We're honored you chose our son to be your forever. We love you, kiddo."

I will not cry. I refuse to mess up the makeup Tamara spent entirely too long doing today.

"Stop it," Tamara snaps at her dad. "I'm not redoing her mascara because you wanted to get all sappy. If you do this tomorrow, I'm going to…"

Her dad laughs. "Baby girl, I promise to behave tomorrow, and fifty-dollar mascara shouldn't run. I think you need better products."

Tamara throws up her hands and groans. "It's the best there is on the market, but it has limits. And Gallo men loving is kryptonite for any type of makeup, even the waterproof kind."

"Everyone out," Asher says from the door.

My eyes move to him, finding him leaning against the doorframe, looking every bit as handsome as he always does. "I need a moment with my wife-to-be."

My stomach flips as the realization finally settles inside me. We're getting married tomorrow. I'm going to be Mrs. Asher Gallo… My teenage girl fantasy is coming true.

The room clears without much grumbling, except from Tamara, but even she doesn't put up too much of a fuss.

"Hey," I say, smiling at my soon-to-be husband.

He strides into the room and holds out his hand as soon as he's in front of me. "Come here," he says softly.

I place my hand in his palm, staring up at him. "Is everything okay?"

He pulls me up and straight into his arms. "Couldn't be better," he says, nuzzling my neck. "I just wanted you to myself instead of sharing you with everyone else."

"You always have me to yourself. Sometimes we need to learn to share well with others."

"I've never been good at sharing."

"Shocking," I whisper, teasing him.

"I saw your parents come in here." He pulls back, staring down at me. "Did it go okay?"

I shrug. "Like it always does. I might as well be talking to the librarian about a random book I want to check out at the library. But it's fine."

"I wish they were different for you."

I smile up at Asher, knowing he's giving me more than I ever could've dreamed. Not only did I get him, but I got everyone else too. "I have your family now. What more could a girl ask for?"

"We're the lucky ones, Oli, not you. My life was empty before you came back to me."

I push up on my tiptoes, brushing my nose against his. "It's where I was always meant to be."

EPILOGUE - ASHER

THREE YEARS LATER...

"Where's my baby boy?" Ma asks as she walks into the house.

"I'm right here," I call out, giving her a big smile.

She shakes her head, not looking amused in the slightest. "You know who I'm talking about."

I sigh.

I was always the baby boy of the family, but that honor has been taken away from me now. All the attention I got before now falls on Lennox, my pride and joy, who's only a few days old.

"Let me have him." Ma reaches for him as my dad stands behind her, staring down at his grandson with so much admiration.

"What about me?" I whine as she takes him from my arms, never losing her touch with the little ones.

"You'll always be my baby, Ash, but Lennox has me wrapped around his tiny little fingers right now."

"Forever," I mutter, but I'm not the least bit salty.

"Stop it," she chides me, bouncing Lennox in her arms as she starts to move around the living room. "He's the most beautiful little thing in the entire world."

I can't argue with her on that. He's stunning. I never knew I could love anything or anyone the way I love him. I'd lay down my life for him, and so would Olive.

"Where's Olive?" Pop asks, glancing around the living room.

"Napping on the patio."

The sound of the waves always lulls her into a deep sleep. Last night, she slept like shit, wanting to be the one to get up with Lennox throughout the night. She's decided to breastfeed him, and that's put most of the burden on her, especially since he's hungry every few hours.

"She's exhausted," I explain, hoping they understand why she's sleeping in the middle of the day. "I thought I'd let her rest."

"Don't wake her," Ma says, swaying Lennox in her arms. "She needs rest. It's not easy being a mother."

"Or a father," I add in there because I feel like we're forgotten. "We do a lot too."

"Hell, I stayed up with you almost every night when you were little, Ash. You were a screamer too."

"He wanted everyone to know he existed, just like his daddy," Ma says to Lennox. "Are you going to be demanding like him or sweet like your momma?"

"Sweet," Olive whispers from the sliding glass doors, rubbing her eyes. "He's not a fuss-bucket like his daddy."

"I'm not a fuss bucket," I say, but I totally am, and I'm okay with it too. I've never been an easy man, and from what my mother is saying, I came out of the womb like that, and it's never left me to this day.

Olive walks slowly toward the couch, careful with every step. She's still sore from giving birth, but she's a trooper. I'd probably be on the floor crying at this point. Lennox almost tore her right down the middle.

"A few more days and you won't hurt as much," Ma tells Olive, watching as she walks. "The men in this family have big heads."

Olive grabs the armrest, careful not to slam down on her middle as she sits. "He was worth it."

"I know I am," I say, teasing her.

Olive eyes me as she tries to get comfortable, but she can't seem to find the right position. "No one ever tells you about the days after you give birth."

"A hot bath does wonders," Ma tells her.

"I'll soak for a while tonight if Lennox can go long enough between feedings."

"Anthony," Ma says, and my father's gaze moves

from Lennox to her. "Get on your phone and order a pump and all the supplies to be delivered today. This girl is going to need a rest eventually or she's going to fall over from lack of sleep."

"I don't know if he'll take a bottle."

"He'll get used to it. It takes some time, but honey," Ma says to Olive, touching her shoulder, "if you don't let yourself get a little rest at night sometimes, you're going to keel over. Self-care is important, sweetheart."

"On it," Pop says, sitting down in the recliner I bought specifically for him.

Ma doesn't stop moving, though. "Why don't you two go nap together? Your dad and I've got this."

I glance at Olive as she yawns. "You think they're trying to get rid of us?"

She gives me a lazy smile, blinking slowly. "I think so."

The front door opens, and my sister strides in with the two kids and Mammoth behind her, carrying a bunch of presents. "We're here," she announces before letting out a loud huff. "Barely, but we are."

Olive instantly perks up a little bit. "I'm so happy you made it."

"The monsters were a little tougher than normal today or else we would've been here earlier," she tells us as she places her purse and shoes next to the door.

"Unkie Ash," Riley says, her little-girl lisp of years ago gone. I never thought I'd miss it, but I do. If I could turn back time and keep her small, I would in a heartbeat. "I brought you a sucker."

I smile at her, holding out my arms for her to run to me like she always does. "That's my girl," I tell her, swallowing her up in a big hug as soon as she's within reach. "I don't need a sucker when I have your hugs, baby girl."

Riley giggles as I kiss her cheek, squealing as she tries to wipe away the wetness left by my lips. "Ew," she screeches, struggling in my arms.

"I was just telling them to go lie down," Ma tells Tamara. "They need rest."

Tamara lets out a grunt. "Can we nap too? Dad can watch Riley and Jackson."

"Hey, Gramps," Jackson says, every bit a little man and looking identical to his father. "What's up?"

"Jack," Pop says, pulling Jackson into his lap even though he's almost too big for that now.

Jackson doesn't put up a struggle, instead making himself comfortable. "Whatcha looking at?" He studies my dad's phone screen.

"Pumps?"

Jackson points at the screen. "What is that?"

"Dad!" Tamara shouts, and my father scrambles, almost throwing his phone.

"What?" Pop says, his eyes wide. "What'd I do?"

"Are you looking at breast pumps?" Tamara asks him.

He sets his phone screen-side down on his leg

that's not occupied by Jackson's ass. "Yeah. Your mother told me to order all the supplies for Olive."

"I don't think Jackson needs to see that."

"I've seen boobs," Jackson tells everyone.

All eyes turn to the little guy.

"What?" he says with a shrug. "They're no big deal."

"You've seen boobs where?" Mammoth asks his son, arms folded in front, looking a little more curious than he usually does.

"The beach."

Mammoth rolls his eyes. "You haven't seen boobs, kid."

"Well, they're just like the ones in the photos Gramps was just looking at."

"I wasn't looking at boobs," Pops says, shifting underneath Jackson. "I was ordering something."

"Something with boobs."

Tamara snickers and covers her mouth when my mother shoots her a salty look. "Jack, can you get Grandma a bottle of water from the fridge?"

Without hesitation, Jackson jumps down from my dad's lap and heads to the kitchen.

"He's going to be a handful when he's older," Ma warns Tamara and Mammoth. "But that's not surprising since you're his parents."

"You started it," Tamara shoots back as she sits on the love seat across from me. "You and Dad weren't the most boring people, and we have your genes."

"I was never boring," Pop says, lifting his chin like he's hurt by the comment. "Your mother may have been, but me…never."

"The kid probably has a nudie magazine stashed away somewhere in his room." I chuckle, thinking about how I used to steal my dad's at a younger age than Jackson. I didn't know what the hell I was looking at, but I knew I liked it.

"No, he doesn't. I've looked," Mammoth tells me. "But it'll happen someday."

Tamara turns her gaze toward him. "Do we have nudie magazines inside the house?"

"What's a nudie magazine?" Riley asks me.

I start to choke on my own saliva. I forget she's old enough to know what we're talking about, and she's filled with a million questions. "It just has pictures," I tell her.

"Like the ones in the bathroom at Big Nonna's house?"

I nod. "Just like those," I lie. They're nothing like *Reader's Digest* and *Good Housekeeping*, but the kid doesn't need to know that.

If I could shelter them from the world forever, I would, but I know it's impossible. Someday, someone out there is going to break Riley's, Jackson's, and even Lennox's little hearts, and it's going to take everything in me not to stalk out of the house and give them every bit of that pain back.

"You better make sure there's none left in the

house," Tamara whispers to Mammoth. "He's at an impressionable age."

"I have. I threw them all out a long time ago and the vintage ones I have, I put in storage at the garage."

Tamara slumps back into the couch. "Having kids is hard as hell. I swear. If I don't have a full head of gray hair in the next few years, it'll be a small miracle."

"Asher found one on his head this morning," Olive tells my sister.

I hate it too. I ripped the thing out by the root and threw it right in the trash can. I'll do that to any others I find until I can't anymore or I'd risk becoming bald.

"Men only grow more handsome with their gray, but us…" Tamara shakes her head and curls her lip, "we somehow look like old maids."

"It's not fair," Olive agrees with her.

"Hair dye, babes, lots and lots of hair dye," Ma tells them. "It's the only way, or else you're going to have to allow yourself to age naturally and gracefully."

"Is it graceful, though?" Tamara asks Ma.

Olive turns to me and grabs my hand. "I love you," she whispers with a smile. "Thank you for this."

"For what?" I ask, but I quickly add, "I love you too."

"For giving me a family," she says, ticking her head toward the others in the room. "All of them."

"You're one of us now, baby. You are and always will be a Gallo Girl."

Do you love the Gallos? They're not over yet!

There's one more story in the Men of Inked Heatwave series. Austin Moore, Pike's brother, is getting a full length book! And he's about to find fall hard for a woman who supposed to be off limits. Grab your copy of **DARE** and be ready for more family fun.

New Series Alert! Soon we're heading back to the Southside of Chicago to catch up with the other side of the Gallo family. Reserve your copy of **CRAVE**, Men of Inked Chicago Book 1. I hope you're ready for the second generation based on the Men of Inked Southside.

Tate Gallo has a wild side, but she's about to meet a man who's all about control. Visit ***menofinked.com/crave*** for more information.

COMING UP NEXT

Annie Hancock is finally following her dreams, studying for her graduate degree to become a professional artist. But when someone starts to leave threatening notes around her studio and dorm, Annie can't help but wonder…who's after her and why? She doesn't know who to trust or keep herself safe.

Arrow has been grinding for years as a bounty hunter and private investigator. After setting down roots and opening his own office, his business doesn't take off the way he'd hoped. Just when he's about to change course, a beautiful woman is in desperate need of his services.

But what starts out as a simple assignment becomes more complicated when they're forced into hiding. And as the threat gets closer, and the attraction becomes hotter, they'll need to decide if what they have is real or driven by danger.

Broken Arrow releases December 5, 2023
Preorder at *menofinked.com/broken-arrow*

Austin Moore found his purpose in the military, but there was always something missing. He wanted what everyone in his family had…someone to call his own. But his life didn't make it easy to find a soul mate, someone to be his forever.

Sage Hill enlisted to follow in the footsteps of her father, but never wanted to be in his shadow. And when her friend ditches her at a dive bar, she catches the eye of a handsome stranger. But Sage doesn't have time for relationships, nor does she want the complication.

When Sage is stuck, Austin tries to be her saving grace and a challenge leads to a lip lock neither one of them can forget. She swore she'd never fall for a strong and bossy man like her father, but she soon learns there's more than meets the eye underneath that sexy exterior.

Part of this book was previously released as the book Fearless. Much of the content has been changed and over 100 pages of new material has been added.

Dare is also part of the Men of Inked world.

Dare releases January 30, 2024
Preorder DARE at ***menofinked.com/dare***

MEN OF INKED CHICAGO #1

When Tate Gallo turned thirty, she swore off three things—drinking, donuts, and dating.

Giving up drinking and dating were easy, but donuts…almost impossible.

But then a handsome man with a wicked grin, hungry eyes, and an interesting proposition makes her question her decision.

Crave releases April 2, 2024

PREORDER CRAVE HERE!

or visit *menofinked.com/crave*

NEED MORE MEN OF INKED?

Have you read the Men of Inked Southside series? Visit ***menofinked.com/southside*** to learn more and be prepared for the Men of Inked Chicago, the next generation, coming Spring 2024!

Book 1 - Broken Sparrow (Morris)
Book 2 - Broken Dove (Leo)
Book 3 - Broken Wings (Crow)
Book 4 - Broken Arrow (Arrow)

To learn more, please visit
menofinked.com/open-road-series

WANT SIGNED PAPERBACKS?

Visit *chelleblissromance.com* for signed paperbacks and book merchandise.

Check out a bigger version at ***menofinked.com/gallo-family-tree*** or view the series reading order at ***menofinked.com/gallo-saga***

Want to be the first to know about the next Men of Inked? Join my newsletter by tapping here to sign up or visit *menofinked.com/inked-news*

Want a place to talk romance books, meet other bookworms, and all things Men of Inked? Join Chelle Bliss Books on Facebook to get sneak peeks, exclusive news, and special giveaways.

Made in the USA
Columbia, SC
30 July 2024

39667418R00188